Monster

Walter Dean Myers

Monster

 HAMPTON-BROWN

This book contains mature content. Educators and parents
should read the book and determine its appropriateness
for use with their students.

Hampton-Brown
P.O. Box 223220
Carmel, California 93922
800-333-3510
www.hampton-brown.com

Printed in the United States of America

ISBN-13: 978-0-7362-3194-7
ISBN-10: 0-7362-3194-3

13 14 15 10 9 8 7 6 5 4 3

To John Brendel
for his long friendship

Introduction

The main character in *Monster*, Steve Harmon, is on trial for his life. Accused of murdering a shopkeeper, Steve tells his story while he is in prison. He writes about his fear of having to spend the rest of his life in jail. Steve also tells about his life before prison, and about his hopes and plans for the future. The readers are like a jury. They must use the facts from the trial and what they learn about Steve from his writing to figure out if he is innocent or guilty.

Before his arrest, Steve planned to be a filmmaker. He made movies about life in the dangerous neighborhood where he lived. Now he writes what is happening in court in the form of a **screenplay** . The screenplay is what writers and filmmakers use to make movies. The author, Walter Dean Myers, wrote the book in this format because of what he learned during his interviews with prisoners. He noticed that many prisoners tried to separate themselves from their crimes—as if the criminal was not a real person but a character in a movie.

Myers' interviews with prisoners was only one part of his research. Myers got more information for *Monster*

Key Concepts

screenplay *n.* the written form of a movie; a movie script

Screenplay Terms	Definitions
Close Up (CU)	A camera shot taken close to a person. The person appears very large.
Cut To	The point when one camera shot immediately changes to another camera shot. The viewer sees one scene stop and another begin.
Fade In	The screen goes from complete black to a fully detailed picture.
Fade Out	The screen goes from a fully detailed picture to compete black.
Flashback	A segment of film that occurs in the past and interrupts the time order of the plot.
Long Shot (LS)	A camera shot taken far from a person. The person appears very small.
Medium Shot (MS)	A camera shot of a person from the waist or knees up.
Pan	A horizontal shot of the setting.
Point-of-View (POV)	A camera shot made from the perspective of one of the characters.
Voice-Over (VO)	A recorded voice that provides narration to the film.

by researching how the United States **judicial** system works. He wanted to know how our laws and procedures would affect his characters. Steve is accused of being part of a store robbery. What makes the crime worse is that the owner of the store is murdered. In our **legal** system, a person is innocent until he or she is proven guilty. Steve is arrested according to the laws of the government. But he cannot be punished without a trial.

On one side of the trial is a **prosecutor**. An accused person like Steve also has a lawyer called a **defense** lawyer. The lawyers argue the case before the judge and jury. The jury is a group of twelve citizens. They listen to the arguments of the lawyers and follow the instructions of the judge. In the end, the jury decides if the accused is innocent or guilty.

The reader learns about Steve as he goes through his trial. Steve may be sent to prison for life. He may even receive the death penalty. Like the jury, the reader must decide. Is Steve a monster who commits a terrible crime? Will the jury find him guilty because of his age and his race? At the same time, Myers raises other important questions: *How does a young boy end up in jail?* and, *Is everyone considered innocent until proven guilty?*

Key Concepts

judicial *adj.* relating to fairness or equality

legal *adj.* relating to rules or law

prosecutor *n.* lawyer who works to prove the person accused is guilty

defense *adj.* kind of lawyer who attempts to prove the person accused is innocent

The best time to cry is at night, when the lights are out and someone is being **beaten up** and screaming for help. That way even if you **sniffle a little** they won't hear you. If anybody knows that you are crying, they'll start talking about it and soon it'll be your turn to get beat up when the lights go out.

There is a mirror over the steel sink in my cell. It's six inches high, and **scratched with** the names of some guys who were here before me. When I look into the small rectangle, I see a face looking back at me but I don't recognize it. It doesn't look like me. I couldn't have changed that much in a few months. I wonder if I will look like myself when **the trial** is over.

This morning at breakfast a guy got hit in the face with a tray. Somebody said some little thing and somebody else got mad. There was blood all over the place.

When the guards came over, they made us line up against the wall. The guy who was hit they made sit at the table while they waited for another guard to

....

beaten up punched and kicked
sniffle a little make noise when you cry
scratched with on it are written
the trial the court case

bring them rubber gloves. When the gloves came, the guards put them on, handcuffed the guy, and then took him to the **dispensary**. He was still bleeding **pretty bad**.

They say you get used to being in jail, but I don't see how. Every morning I wake up and I am surprised to be here. If your life outside was real, then everything in here is just the opposite. We sleep with strangers, wake up with strangers, and go to the bathroom in front of strangers. They're strangers but they still find reasons to hurt each other.

Sometimes I feel like I have walked into the middle of a movie. It is a strange movie with no **plot** and no beginning. The movie is in black and white, and **grainy**. Sometimes the camera moves in so close that you can't tell what is going on and you just listen to the sounds and guess. I have seen movies of prisons but never one like this. This is not a movie about bars and locked doors. It is about being alone when you are not really alone and about being scared all the time.

....

dispensary hospital; medical center
pretty bad a lot; badly
plot story
grainy blurry; not clear

I think to get used to this I will have to give up what I think is real and **take up** something else. I wish I could make sense of it.

Maybe I could make my own movie. I could write it out and play it in my head. I could **block out** the scenes like we did in school. The film will be the story of my life. No, not my life, but of this experience. I'll write it down in the notebook they **let me keep**. I'll call it what the lady who is the prosecutor called me.

MONSTER

....

take up start believing in
block out plan, organize
let me keep allow me to have; let me write in

Monster!

FADE IN: INTERIOR: Early morning in CELL BLOCK D, MANHATTAN DETENTION CENTER. Camera goes slowly down **grim**, gray corridor. There are sounds of **inmates** yelling from cell to cell; much of it is obscene. Most of the voices are clearly Black or Hispanic. Camera stops and slowly turns toward a cell.

INTERIOR: CELL. Sixteen-year-old STEVE HARMON is sitting on the edge of a metal cot, head in hands. He is thin, brown skinned. On the **cot** next to him are the suit and tie he is to wear to court for the start of his trial.

CUT TO: ERNIE, another prisoner, sitting on **john**, pants down.

CUT TO: SUNSET, another prisoner, pulling on T-shirt.

CUT TO: STEVE pulling blanket over his head as screen goes dark.

....

grim sad, lonely
inmates people in jail; prisoners
cot small bed
john the toilet

VOICE-OVER (VO): Ain't no use putting the blanket over your head, man. You can't cut this out; this is reality. This is the real deal.

VO continues with anonymous PRISONER explaining how the Detention Center is the real thing. As he does, words appear on the screen, just like the opening credits of the movie **Star Wars**, rolling from the bottom of the screen and shrinking until they are a blur on the top of the screen before rolling off into space.

Monster!
The Story of
My
Miserable
Life

Starring
Steve Harmon

Produced by
Steve Harmon

Directed by
Steve Harmon

(Credits continue to roll.)

The incredible story *of how* one guy's life *was* turned around *by a* few events *and* how he might *spend* the rest of his life behind bars.

Told as it

actually happened!

Written and directed by Steve Harmon

Featuring . . .

Sandra Petrocelli
as the Dedicated Prosecutor

Kathy O'Brien
as the Defense Attorney with Doubts

James King
as the Thug

Richard "Bobo" Evans
as the Rat

Osvaldo Cruz, member of the Diablos,
as the Tough Guy Wannabe

Lorelle Henry
as the Witness

José Delgado . . .
he found the body

And Starring

16-year-old Steve Harmon
as the Boy on Trial for Murder!

Filmed at the Manhattan Detention Center

**Set design, handcuffs, and prison outfits by
the State of New York**

VO: Yo, Harmon, you gonna eat something? Come on and get your breakfast, man. I'll take your eggs if you don't want them. You want them?

STEVE (subdued): I'm not hungry.

SUNSET: His trial starts today. **He up for the big one.** I know how that feels.

CUT TO: INTERIOR: CORRECTIONS DEPT. VAN. Through the bars at the rear of the van, we see people going about the business of

....

Set design The way the scenery looks

subdued quietly

He up for the big one. He is on trial for murder.

CORRECTIONS DEPT. JAIL, PRISON

their lives in downtown New York. There are men collecting garbage, a female traffic officer motioning for a taxi to make a turn, students on the way to school. Few people notice the van as it makes its way from the DETENTION CENTER to the COURTHOUSE.

CUT TO: PRISONERS, handcuffed, coming from back of van. STEVE is carrying a notebook. He is dressed in the suit and tie we saw on the cot. He is seen only briefly as he is herded through the heavy doors of the courthouse.

FADE OUT as last prisoner from the van enters rear of courthouse.

FADE IN: INTERIOR COURTHOUSE. We are in a small room used for prisoner-lawyer interviews. A guard sits at a desk behind STEVE.

KATHY O'BRIEN, STEVE's lawyer, is petite, red-haired, and freckled. She is all business as she talks to STEVE.

O'BRIEN: Let me make sure you understand what's going on. Both you and this King character are on trial for **felony murder.** Felony murder is as serious as it gets. Sandra Petrocelli is the prosecutor, and she's good. **They're pushing for** the death penalty, which is really bad. The jury might think they're doing you a big favor by giving you life in prison. So you'd better take this trial very, very seriously.

....

all business serious, professional

felony murder killing someone while committing a serious crime

They're pushing for The prosecutor wants you to get

When you're in court, you sit there and you pay attention. You let the jury know that you think the case is as serious as they do. You don't turn and wave to any of your friends. It's all right to acknowledge your mother.

I have to go and talk to the judge. The trial will begin in a few minutes. Is there anything you want to ask me before it starts?

STEVE: You think we're going to win?

O'BRIEN (seriously): It probably depends on what you mean by "win."

CUT TO: INTERIOR: **HOLDING ROOM**. We see STEVE sitting at one end of bench. Against the opposite wall, dressed in a sloppy-looking suit, is 23-year-old JAMES KING, the other man on trial. KING looks older than 23. He looks over at STEVE with a **hard look** and we see STEVE look away. Two GUARDS sit at a table away from the prisoners, who are handcuffed. The camera finds the GUARDS in a MEDIUM SHOT (MS). They have their breakfast in aluminum take-out trays that contain eggs, sausages, and potatoes. A Black female **STENOGRAPHER** pours coffee for herself and the GUARDS.

STENOGRAPHER: I hope this case lasts two weeks. I can sure use the money.

....

HOLDING ROOM WHERE PRISONERS WAIT
hard look tough expression on his face
STENOGRAPHER COURT WORKER WHO RECORDS EVERYTHING SAID IN COURT

GUARD 1: Six days—maybe seven. It's a motion case. They go through the motions; then they lock them up.

(Turns and looks off camera toward STEVE.)

Ain't that right, bright eyes?

CUT TO: STEVE, who is seated on a low bench. He is handcuffed to a U-bolt put in the bench for that purpose. STEVE looks away from the GUARD.

CUT TO: DOOR. It opens, and **COURT CLERK** looks in.

COURT CLERK: Two minutes!

CUT TO: GUARDS, who hurriedly finish breakfast. STENOGRAPHER takes machine into COURTROOM.
They **unshackle** STEVE and take him toward door.

CUT TO: STEVE is made to sit down at one table. At another table we see KING and two attorneys. STEVE sits alone.
A guard stands behind him. There are one or two spectators in the court. Then four more enter.

CLOSE-UP (CU) of STEVE HARMON. The fear is evident on his face.

MS: People are getting ready for the trial to begin.
KATHY O'BRIEN sits next to STEVE.

....

COURT CLERK THE COURTROOM MANAGER
unshackle remove the handcuffs from

O'BRIEN: How are you doing?

STEVE: I'm scared.

O'BRIEN: Good; you should be. Anyway, just remember what we've been talking about. The judge is going to rule on a motion that King's lawyer made **to suppress Cruz's testimony**, and a few other things. Steve, let me tell you what my job is here. My job is to make sure the law works for you as well as against you, and to make you a human being in the eyes of the jury. Your job is to help me. Any questions you have, write them down and I'll try to answer them. What are you doing there?

STEVE: I'm writing this whole thing down as a movie.

O'BRIEN: Whatever. Make sure you pay attention. Close attention.

VO (COURT GUARD): **All rise.**

The JUDGE enters and sits behind **bench**. He is tall and thin. He pushes his fingers through wisps of white hair and looks over the COURTROOM before sitting. He is a 60-year-old New York judge and already looks bored with the case. The COURT GUARD signals for people to sit.

....

to suppress Cruz's testimony that would not allow the jury to hear what Cruz said

All rise. Everyone stand.

bench a large desk

JUDGE: Prosecution ready?

SANDRA PETROCELLI, the prosecutor, stands. She is dressed in a gray business suit. She looks intense while still being attractive. Her hair and eyes are dark.

PETROCELLI: Ready, **Your Honor.**

JUDGE: Defense?

ASA BRIGGS, the **lead counsel for** the defense of JAMES KING, stands. He is dressed in a dark-blue suit and a light-blue tie. His eyes are also blue, and his hair is white.

BRIGGS: Ready.

O'BRIEN: Ready, Your Honor.

JUDGE: All right. **I'm ruling the kid's testimony is admissible.** You can bring up your motions relative to that ruling this afternoon or if there's a break. Hope everyone had a good Fourth of July?

BRIGGS: The usual barbecue and a softball game that reminded me that I can't run anymore.

....

Your Honor Judge

lead counsel for lawyer in charge of

I'm ruling the kid's testimony is admissible. My decision is that the jury can hear what Cruz said about the crime.

O'BRIEN: With all the fireworks, it's my least favorite holiday.

JUDGE: Bring in the jury.

CUT TO: FILM WORKSHOP at Stuyvesant High School. A film on a small screen is just ending. It is a class project, and the camera is shaky. We watch as a girl on the screen walks slowly away. Screen goes black, then dazzling white, then normal as lights go on.

We see MR. SAWICKI, **film club mentor**, and 9 STUDENTS, who are casually dressed.

SAWICKI: In a **juried competition** the ending would have hurt this piece, but otherwise it was interesting. Any comments?

We see STEVE raising his hand, looking much the same as he does in court.

STEVE: I liked the ending.

SAWICKI: I didn't say it was bad, but wasn't it **predictable**? You need to predict without

....

film club mentor leader of the school film group
juried competition contest where a jury chooses the winner
predictable easy to know what would happen

predicting. You know what I mean? When you make a film, you **leave an impression** on the viewers, who serve as a kind of jury for your film. If you make your film predictable, they'll make up their minds about it long before it's over.

....

leave an impression make an impact

BEFORE YOU MOVE ON...

1. **Comparisons** How is the diary different from the screenplay? Compare how they look, how they tell the story, and how they make you feel.

2. **Inference** Reread pages 20–21. What do people think of Steve? How do you know?

LOOK AHEAD Read pages 26–42 to see how Steve feels about himself.

CUT TO: COURTROOM. We see the JURORS filing in and taking their seats.

STEVE (to attorney): You think they look all right?

O'BRIEN: They are what we have for a jury. We have to **deal with them**.

CUT TO: LONG SHOT (LS) of PETROCELLI. She stands at the podium in front of the JURY. She smiles at the JURORS, and some smile back.

PETROCELLI: Good morning, ladies and gentlemen. My name is Sandra Petrocelli and I'm an Assistant District Attorney for the State of New York. I am **representing the people in this matter**, which you were informed during jury selection is a case of felony murder. We're here today basically because this is not a perfect world. The founding fathers of our country understood this. They knew that there would be times and circumstances during which our society would be threatened by the acts of individuals. This is one of those times. A citizen of our city, a citizen of our state and country, has been killed by people who **attempted** to rob him. To

....

deal with them work with them whether we like it or not
representing the people in this matter speaking for the people of New York about this crime
attempted tried

26

safeguard our society, a system of laws has been created. You, the jury, are part of this system of laws. I represent the State of New York and I am part of that system, as are the judge and all the participants in this trial. I will do my best to bring you the facts of this case, and I know you will do your best to **judge the merits** of the case.

Most people in our community are decent, hardworking citizens who pursue their own interests legally and without **infringing on** the rights of others. But there are also monsters in our communities—people who are willing to steal and to kill, people who **disregard** the rights of others.

On the 22nd of December of last year, at approximately 4 o'clock in the afternoon, 2 men entered a drugstore on 145th Street in Harlem. The State **will contend** that one of those men was Richard "Bobo" Evans. The State will contend that the other man who entered the store at that time, and who participated in the robbery and the murder, was James King.

PETROCELLI points to the table at which JAMES KING sits.

....

judge the merits make decisions based on facts
infringing on taking away
disregard choose to ignore
will contend believes; will prove

Mr. King is the man sitting at that table who is wearing a brown suit and is sitting at the right of the table. You were introduced to him during the jury selection process. He is one of the men on trial here today. The **purpose of** the 2 men entering the store on that Monday was very simple. They were going to rob the owner, 55-year-old Alguinaldo Nesbitt. We will show that although the 2 men did not have a gun with them, the owner of the store did have a gun for which he had a license, and **produced it** to defend his property.

Mr. Evans, who participated in the robbery, will testify that there was a struggle, which resulted in the gun being **discharged** and Mr. Nesbitt being killed. Mr. Nesbitt had every right to defend his property, every right not to be robbed. We all have that right.

Further, there will be evidence that prior to the robbery there was a plan, or conspiracy, to rob the store. Mr. Evans and Mr. King were to enter the store and do the actual robbery. Another of the planners of this crime was to stand outside the drugstore and **impede** anyone chasing the robbers. The young man who had this assignment will testify to his role in

....

purpose of reason for
produced it he took out the gun
discharged shot, used
impede stop

the affair. Yet another of the conspirators, the planners of this robbery that left a man dead, was to go into the store prior to the robbery to check it out, to make sure that there were no police in the store. To make sure that the coast was clear, as they say.

Two of the conspirators will testify to their understanding of this fact. The man who was to enter the store and check it out is sitting at the other table. His name is Steven Harmon.

CUT TO: STEVE HARMON. Then: CU of the pad in front of him. He is writing the word *Monster* over and over again. A white hand (O'BRIEN's) takes the pencil from his hand and crosses out all the *Monsters*.

O'BRIEN (whispering): You have to believe in yourself if we're going to convince a jury that you're innocent.

CUT TO: MS of PETROCELLI.

PETROCELLI: A **medical examiner** will testify to the cause of death, showing that the gunshot wound **was fatal**. Even though it was Mr. Nesbitt's gun, it was not Mr. Nesbitt who caused his own death. This was no suicide. This death was a direct result of the robbery.

....

medical examiner doctor who looked at Mr. Nesbitt's dead body

was fatal killed him

Very simply put, this is a case of murder. It is, moreover, a murder committed during **a felonious act.** The 2 **defendants** you see before you will be shown to be participants in that act and are being charged with felony murder. Later, the judge will give you instructions on how to consider the evidence presented. But there is no doubt in my mind, and I believe by the end of the trial there will be little doubt in yours, that these 2 men, James King and Steven Harmon, were all part of the robbery that caused the death of Alguinaldo Nesbitt. Thank you.

CUT TO: LS of COURTROOM. O'BRIEN is at attorneys' podium.

CUT TO: STEVE's MOTHER, on wooden bench in **the gallery area**, listening intently. Her face looks worried.

O'BRIEN: The State correctly says that the laws of a society provide protection for its citizens. When a crime is committed, it is the State that must apply the law in a manner that offers **redress** and that brings the guilty parties to justice. But the laws also protect the accused, and that is the wonder and beauty of the American system of justice. We don't drag people out of their beds in the

....

a felonious act another serious crime
defendants people accused of the crime that
the gallery area the section where spectators sit
redress a way to make things fair

middle of the night and lynch them. We don't torture people. We don't beat them. We apply the law equally to both sides. The law that protects society protects all of society. In this case we will show that the evidence that the State will produce **is seriously flawed.** We will show not only that there is room for reasonable doubt—and you will hear more about that idea at the end of this trial—but that the doubt that Steve Harmon has committed any crime, any crime at all, is **overwhelming.**

As Mr. Harmon's attorney all I ask of you, the jury, is that you look at Steve Harmon now and remember that at this moment the American system of justice demands that you consider him innocent. He is innocent until proven guilty. If you consider him innocent now, and by law you must, if you have not **prejudged** him, then I don't believe we will have a problem convincing you that nothing the State will produce will challenge that innocence. Thank you.

CUT TO: BRIGGS.

BRIGGS: Good morning, ladies and gentlemen. My name is Asa Briggs, and I will be defending

....

is seriously flawed has problems
overwhelming too much to ignore
prejudged already made a decision about

Mr. King. Miss Petrocelli, representing the State, has presented this case in **very broad and grandiose terms**. But you will soon see that her key witnesses are among the most self-serving, heartless people imaginable. Some of them will begin their testimony by swearing that they are criminals. You will have the unpleasant task of listening to people who have committed crimes, who have lied and stolen, and in at least one instance has been an admitted, and let me emphasize this, an admitted accomplice to murder. But in the end you will have the opportunity to judge the State's key witnesses and to **deliver a just verdict**. What I am asking you to do is just that. Judge what they bring up on the witness stand, and then deliver your just verdict. Thank you.

CUT TO: WITNESS STAND. JOSÉ DELGADO is on the stand. He is young, very well built, and **articulate**.

JOSÉ: I'm on until 9—the store closes at 9. So in the afternoon I either go home and **grab a bite or go out for Chinese**. That night I went out for Chinese. Usually I get something and

....

very broad and grandiose terms overly important words
deliver a just verdict make a fair decision
articulate speaks well
grab a bite or go out for Chinese eat, or go get Chinese food

eat it in the back. When I went out, everything was okay.

PETROCELLI: What time did you leave the drugstore?

JOSÉ: Four thirty, maybe 4:35 at the latest.

PETROCELLI: And what did you discover on your return?

JOSÉ: At first I didn't see anything—which I knew was weird because Mr. Nesbitt wouldn't leave the place empty. I went around behind the counter and I saw Mr. Nesbitt on the floor—there was blood everywhere—and the cash register was open. A lot of cigarettes were missing, too. Maybe 5 cartons.

PETROCELLI: And did you call the police?

JOSÉ: Yeah, but I knew Mr. Nesbitt was dead.

PETROCELLI: Mr. Delgado, **are you familiar with the so-called martial arts**?

JOSÉ: That's **my hobby. I have a black belt in karate.**

....

are you familiar with the so-called martial arts do you know about a kind of fighting called martial arts

my hobby an activity I do for fun

I have a black belt in karate. I have the highest level of skill in that kind of fighting.

PETROCELLI: Is that fact pretty well known in the neighborhood in which the drugstore **operated**?

JOSÉ: Yeah, because whenever I was in a match and **it made the papers**, Mr. Nesbitt used to put the paper in the window.

PETROCELLI: Did police ever visit the drugstore?

JOSÉ: Sometimes they would come in and sneak a smoke.

PETROCELLI: Nothing further.

BRIGGS: You state that 5 cartons of cigarettes were missing?

JOSÉ: That's right.

BRIGGS: Five, not 6?

JOSÉ: Afterward I checked the **inventory**. It was 5.

BRIGGS: What medical school did you attend?

JOSÉ: None.

....

operated was located and in business
it made the papers it was printed in the newspapers
Nothing further. I do not have any more questions.
inventory list of things we sold in the store

BRIGGS: But you said you knew that Mr. Nesbitt was dead. You were sure of it. That right?

JOSÉ: Pretty sure.

BRIGGS: Sure enough to stop and do inventory before trying to help your boss?

JOSÉ: I didn't take inventory right away, I just noticed. You work in a store, you notice if something is missing.

BRIGGS: How long did it take?

JOSÉ (pissed): I don't remember.

BRIGGS: Nothing further.

O'BRIEN: No questions.

PETROCELLI (as JOSÉ steps down): The state **calls** Salvatore Zinzi.

CUT TO: SAL ZINZI on the stand. He is nervous, slightly overweight. He wears thick glasses, which he touches over and over again as he testifies.

PETROCELLI: Mr. Zinzi, where were you when you first became involved with this case?

....

calls would like to talk with

ZINZI: Riker's Island.

PETROCELLI: Why were you there?

ZINZI: Stolen property. A guy sold me some baseball cards. They were stolen.

PETROCELLI: You knew they were stolen?

ZINZI: Yeah. I guess.

PETROCELLI: While you were at Riker's Island, did you engage in a certain conversation with a Wendell Bolden?

ZINZI: Yes, ma'am.

PETROCELLI: You want to tell me about the conversation?

ZINZI: He said he knew about a drugstore **holdup** where a guy was killed, and he was thinking of **turning the guy in to get a break**.

PETROCELLI: And what did you do as a result of this conversation?

ZINZI: I called Detective Gluck and told him what I knew.

....

Riker's Island. In a jail in New York.

holdup robbery

turning the guy in to get a break telling the police about the robber to get out of jail sooner

PETROCELLI: Because you wanted a break, too. Is that right?

ZINZI: Yeah.

PETROCELLI: So Bolden told you he knew about the crime. Was there anything else?

ZINZI: That was it.

PETROCELLI: Did he tell you about some cigarettes?

ZINZI: Yeah, he—

BRIGGS: Objection! She's leading.

PETROCELLI: Withdrawn. What else did he tell you?

ZINZI: That he got some cigarettes from this guy. Two cartons.

PETROCELLI: Did he tell you the name of the person he got the cigarettes from?

ZINZI: No, just that he was sure the guy was involved in the holdup.

PETROCELLI: Nothing further.

....

Objection! She's leading. I disagree with her question! She is telling the witness what to say.

Withdrawn. I will not ask that question.

CUT TO: BRIGGS at the podium.

BRIGGS: You wanted a break, Mr. Zinzi. Why did you need a break? You only **had a few months to do**; isn't that right?

ZINZI: Some guys were . . . sexually harassing me, sir.

BRIGGS: Sexually harassing? Were they **calling you a sissy**? What does "sexually harass" mean to you?

ZINZI: They wanted to have sex with me.

BRIGGS: So to save yourself from being gang raped—Is that what they wanted to do to you?

ZINZI: Yeah.

BRIGGS: And you were afraid?

ZINZI: Yeah.

BRIGGS: You were afraid, and you would have said just about anything to get out of that situation. Isn't that right?

ZINZI: I guess so.

....

had a few months to do had to be in jail a few months more
calling you a sissy saying you were like a girl

BRIGGS: Would you lie?

ZINZI: No.

BRIGGS: Let me **get this straight**, Mr. Zinzi. You'd buy **stolen goods for profit, rat on somebody to save your own hide**, but you're too good to lie. Is that right?

ZINZI: I'm not lying now.

BRIGGS: As a matter of fact, this Bolden was going to see what he could get out of this, but you **stole his chance, too.** Didn't you?

ZINZI: I guess.

BRIGGS: No further questions.

O'BRIEN: Mr. Zinzi, how long were you in jail?

ZINZI: Forty-three days.

O'BRIEN: Do people in jail look for stories to report to the police?

PETROCELLI (calmly): Objection. The question's too vague.

---

get this straight try to understand this

stolen goods for profit, rat on somebody to save your own hide items that were stolen and then tell the police who the criminal was to save yourself

stole his chance, too went to the police before Bolden did

O'BRIEN: Well, let me put it this way, Mr. Zinzi. This Mr. Bolden was going to use this story **for his own benefit**, is that right?

ZINZI: Right.

O'BRIEN: And you decided to use it for your benefit?

ZINZI: Right. Lots of guys in jail do that.

O'BRIEN: You use stories and you use people, right?

ZINZI: Sometimes.

O'BRIEN: And the outcome of your talking with the detective in question is that you were able to reach the District Attorney's office and **strike a deal**. Isn't that right? You were able to strike a deal that got you out of jail early? Isn't that right?

ZINZI: That's right.

O'BRIEN: You happy with the deal?

ZINZI: Yeah.

O'BRIEN: Nothing further.

....

for his own benefit to help himself

strike a deal make the District Attorney agree to let you out of jail if you testified

PETROCELLI: Mr. Zinzi, do you know when you're lying and when you're telling the truth?

ZINZI: Yes—sure.

PETROCELLI: You telling the truth now?

ZINZI: Yeah.

PETROCELLI: Nothing further.

FLASHBACK of 12-year-old STEVE walking in a NEIGHBORHOOD PARK with his friend TONY.

TONY: They should let me pitch. I can throw **straight as anything.** (Scoops up a rock.) See the lamppost? (Throws rock. We see that it bounces in front of the post and **careens** slightly to one side.)

STEVE: You can't throw. (Picks up rock and throws it. We see it **sail** past the post and hit a YOUNG WOMAN. The TOUGH GUY she is walking with turns and sees the 2 young boys.)

TOUGH GUY: Hey, man. Who threw that rock? (He approaches.)

STEVE: Tony! Run!

....

straight as anything really well
careens moves, falls
sail fly, move

TONY (taking **a tentative** step): What? (TOUGH GUY punches TONY. TONY falls—TOUGH GUY stands over TONY as STEVE **backs off.** YOUNG WOMAN pulls TOUGH GUY away, and they leave.)

TONY and STEVE are left in the park with TONY sitting on the ground.

TONY: I didn't throw that rock. You threw it.

STEVE: I didn't say you threw it. I just said "Run." You should've run.

TONY: I'll get me an Uzi and blow his brains out.

....

a tentative an unsure; an uncertain

backs off moves away

I'll get me an Uzi and blow his brains out. I will get a huge gun and kill him.

BEFORE YOU MOVE ON...

1. **Assumption** What does Steve assume that makes him write the word "monster" over and over again in his notebook?

2. **Flashback** Steve recalls how his friend was blamed for throwing a rock that Steve threw. Why do you think the author included this?

LOOK AHEAD Read pages 43–52 to see Steve's movie flash back to the robbery plans.

Tuesday, July 7th

Notes:

I can hardly think about the movie, I hate this place so much. But if I didn't think of the movie I would go crazy. All they talk about in here is hurting people. If you look at somebody, they say, "What you looking at me for? **I'll mess you up!**" If you make a noise they don't like, they say they'll mess you up. One guy has a knife. It's not really a knife, but a blade glued onto a toothbrush handle.

I hate this place. I hate this place. I can't write it enough times to make it look the way I feel! I <u>hate</u>, —<u>hate</u>, <u>hate</u> this place!!

....

I'll mess you up! I will beat you up!; I will hurt you!

CUT TO: INTERIOR: COURTROOM. WENDELL BOLDEN is on the stand. He is average height but heavily built with large, ashy hands. He acts like he's mad and wants everybody to know it.

PETROCELLI: Mr. Bolden, have you ever been arrested?

BOLDEN: Yeah. For B & E, and possession with intent.

PETROCELLI: Possession is obviously drugs and the intent to distribute. Can you tell the jury what B & E means?

BOLDEN: B & E. **Breaking and entering.**

PETROCELLI: And what were you in for when you spoke to Mr. Zinzi?

BOLDEN: Assault.

PETROCELLI: But the charges were dropped?

BOLDEN: Yeah, they were dropped.

PETROCELLI: Can you tell us about the conversation between you and Mr. Zinzi?

BOLDEN: I got some cigarettes from a guy who told me he was in on a drugstore robbery up

....

Possession is obviously drugs and the intent to distribute.
You were caught with drugs that you wanted to sell.

Breaking and entering. Using force to enter a house.

But the charges were dropped? They decided not to punish you for the charges?

on Malcolm X Boulevard. I knew a **dude** got killed, and I was thinking of trading what I knew for **some slack.**

PETROCELLI: As a matter of fact, didn't Mr. Zinzi also try to use that information himself?

BOLDEN: He called a detective he knew.

PETROCELLI: Can you name the person involved in the robbery?

BRIGGS: Objection! He can testify to the conversation—not the robbery, unless he was there.

PETROCELLI: Withdrawn. . . . So who gave you the information that he was involved in a robbery?

BOLDEN: Bobo Evans.

Camera pans to KING, who gives BOLDEN a dirty look.

CUT TO: EXTERIOR STOOP ON 141ST STREET. There is a small tricycle on the sidewalk. It is missing one wheel. The garbage cans at the curb are overflowing. Three young girls jump rope near the trash.

....

dude man who
some slack less time in jail

JAMES KING and STEVE are sitting on the steps. A heavy woman, PEACHES, sits slightly above them, and a thin man, JOHNNY, stands. He is smoking a blunt.

KING (almost a drawl): I need to get paid, man. I ain't got nothing between my butt and the ground but a rag.

STEVE: I hear that.

PEACHES: You can't even hardly make it these days. They talking about cutting welfare, cutting Social Security, and anything else that makes life a little easy. They might as well bring back slavery times if you ask me.

KING: If I had a crew, I could get paid. All you need is a crew with some heart and **a nose for the cash**.

PEACHES: Banks is where the money is.

JOHNNY: Naw. Bank money is too serious. **The man comes down hard for bank money.** You need to find a **getover** where nobody don't care—you know what I mean. You **cop** from somebody with a green card or an illegal and they don't even report it.

....

a nose for the cash a sense for which place to rob

The man comes down hard for bank money. The police punish bank robbers with a lot of jail time.

getover place to rob

cop steal

PEACHES: Restaurant owners got money, too. That's the only things left in our neighborhood—restaurants, liquor stores, and drugstores.

KING: What you got, youngblood?

STEVE (Looks up at KING.)**:** I don't know.

JOHNNY: Yo—what's your name? Steve. Since when **you been down**?

CUT TO: INTERIOR: COURTROOM. BOLDEN is still on the stand.

BOLDEN: So he **turned me on to** 2 cartons for 5 dollars each. I asked him how he copped and he said he was in a robbery in a drugstore. I didn't say no more because all I wanted was the smokes.

PETROCELLI: Did he tell you when the store was robbed?

BOLDEN: He said it just went down.

PETROCELLI: And when did this conversation take place?

....

What you got, youngblood? Do you have any ideas?
you been down have you wanted to be a criminal
turned me on to told me I could buy

BOLDEN: The day before Christmas. I remember that because I gave a carton of cigarettes to my moms as a present.

PETROCELLI: No further questions.

BRIGGS: How well do you know Mr. Evans?

BOLDEN: I know him when I see him.

BRIGGS: Did you know him before Christmas?

BOLDEN: Not really.

BRIGGS: Let's see, now. You don't know this man, and yet when you ask him where he got the cigarettes, he's going to tell you that he got them from a holdup in which he was involved and in which a man was killed?

BOLDEN: If he wants to **run his mouth**, that's his business.

BRIGGS: And didn't you think it strange that a man would give out information that could be harmful to him if he had actually been involved in this case?

CUT TO: CU of JUROR looking bored.

....

I know him when I see him. I do not know him except to see him around town.

run his mouth tell me things

CUT TO: CU of BOLDEN.

BOLDEN: Hey, I don't even care.

BRIGGS: Your assault charge was dropped—is that correct?

BOLDEN: Yeah.

BRIGGS: The **maximum sentence** for the assault was how long? Do you know?

BOLDEN: I wasn't **convicted**.

BRIGGS: Do you know the maximum sentence?

PETROCELLI: Objection.

JUDGE: Overruled; it's **pertinent**.

BRIGGS: So you saved yourself some heavy jail time by **pointing a finger at** Mr. King, isn't that right?

BOLDEN: I just wanted to do the right thing. You know, like a good citizen.

BRIGGS (showing anger): You were in jail trying to be a good citizen? Or were you really just trying to get out of jail and not

----

maximum sentence longest jail time you could have received
convicted given a guilty verdict
pertinent important to this case
pointing a finger at blaming, accusing

caring who you **put in**? Isn't that what you're really doing? Well, isn't it?

PETROCELLI: Objection! Defense counsel is **stepping over his bounds**.

JUDGE: This is a good time for a break. I have some administrative tasks to get done this afternoon. Let's **adjourn** until tomorrow. I want to remind the jury not to discuss the case with anyone. We'll **reconvene** 9 A.M. tomorrow.

CUT TO: INTERIOR: DETENTION CENTER. It is night; the lights are out except for dim night-lights placed along the walls. We hear the sounds of fists methodically punching someone as the camera goes slowly down the corridor, almost seeming to look for the source of the hitting. We see two inmates silhouetted, beating a third. Another inmate is on lookout.

CUT TO: CU of STEVE lying on his cot. The sounds are in his cell, but he is not the one being beaten. We see the whites of his eyes, then we see him close his eyes as the sounds of the beating stop and the sounds become those of a sexual attack against the inmate who was beaten.

FADE OUT.

....

put in put in jail with your testimony
stepping over his bounds saying things he should not say
adjourn stop the trial; postpone the rest of the trial
reconvene begin the trial again at

FADE IN: INTERIOR: STEVE's HOME. It **is neatly furnished**, clean. STEVE is watching TV with 11 year-old JERRY, his brother.

JERRY: You ever want to be a superhero? You know, save people and stuff?

STEVE: Sure. You know who I'd want to be? Superman. I'd be wearing glasses and stuff and people would be **messing with me and then I'd kick butt.**

JERRY: I bet you'd be a cool superhero. You know who you should be?

STEVE: Who?

JERRY: Batman. Then I could be Robin. (STEVE gives JERRY a **brotherly shove**.)

FADE OUT.

....

is neatly furnished has nice furniture

messing with me and then I'd kick butt trying to hurt me and then I would beat them up

brotherly shove little push that is meant to be a joke

BEFORE YOU MOVE ON...

1. **Conflict** Reread pages 46–47. Why does Steve stay quiet while his neighbors are making plans to steal money?

2. **Character** Reread page 52. What does this flashback show about Steve?

LOOK AHEAD Read pages 53–64 to see why Steve feels more and more like he's just a character in a movie.

Wednesday, July 8th

They take away your shoelaces and your belt so you can't kill yourself no matter how bad it is. I guess making you live is part of the punishment.

It's funny but when I'm sitting in the courtroom, I don't feel like I'm involved in the case. It's like the lawyers and judge and everybody are doing a job that involves me, but I don't **have a role.** It's only when I go back to the cells that I know I'm involved.

Miss O'Brien says that Petrocelli is using Bolden's testimony as part of a trail that will lead to me and James King. I think she is wrong. I think they are bringing out all of these people and letting them look terrible on the stand and sound terrible and then reminding the jury that they don't look any different from me and King.

I like the last scene in the movie, the one between me and Jerry. It makes me seem like a real person.

The man they called Sunset asked me if he could

---

have a role participate at all

read the screenplay, and I let him. He liked it. Sunset said he liked the name of the screenplay. He said when he gets out, he will have the word Monster **tattooed** on his forehead. I feel like I already have it tattooed on mine.

A preacher came to the recreation room with a guard this afternoon. He asked if anyone wanted to talk to him or share a moment of prayer. Two guys said they did, and I was just about ready to say I would when Lynch, a guy who is going on trial for killing his wife, started **cursing** at the preacher and saying that everybody wanted to talk to him and act like they were good when they were just criminals. "It's too late to **put up your holy front now**," he said.

In a way he was right, at least about me. I want to look like a good person. I want to feel like I'm a good person because I believe I am. But being in here with these guys makes it hard to think about yourself as being different. We look about the same, and even though I'm younger than they are, it's hard not to notice that we are all pretty young. I see what Miss

....

tattooed permanently written

cursing saying bad words

put up your holy front now act like you are religious now; behave like you are good

O'Brien meant when she said part of her job was to make me look human **in the eyes of** the jury.

When Lynch started cursing at the preacher, the guards took the preacher out, and then they came back and turned the television off and made us go back to our cells.

Notes:

I couldn't sleep most of the night after the dream. The dream took place in the courtroom. I was trying to ask questions and nobody could hear me. I was shouting and shouting but everyone went about their business as if I wasn't there. I hope I didn't shout out in my sleep. That would look weak to everybody. It's not good to be weak in here.

Every morning we get up and put on our court clothes. The talk is **lawyer talk**, with all the older guys talking about **appeals** and "mistakes" that the judge made.

I feel terrible. My stomach is gassy and **bloated**. I still can't go to the bathroom in front of everyone.

....

in the eyes of in front of
lawyer talk discussion of what is happening in court
appeals asking for another trial
bloated swollen, puffy

When we got in the court, there was a delay because the stenographer had brought the wrong **power cord.** The court officer was talking about termites.

....

power cord electrical cord to turn on the machine

FADE IN: COURTROOM. STEVE and KING are cuffed to a bench. COURT OFFICERS, PETROCELLI, STENOGRAPHER, JUDGE, BRIGGS, and O'BRIEN are present.

OFFICER 1: So this guy comes to the house and tells Vivian we got termites. I get home and she's all upset. I said no way we got termites. No way.

JUDGE: You ever see any termites?

OFFICER 1: What the heck's a termite look like?

O'BRIEN: Like an ant with wings.

OFFICER 1: Then I've never seen one.

OFFICER 2: I heard they hide in the wood.

JUDGE: What I don't understand is why they have wings if they stay in the wood.

PETROCELLI: Are you going to let us **do the affidavit on** the crime scene?

JUDGE: Any objections?

BRIGGS: Who's going to read it in court?

....

do the affidavit on read the detective's description of what he saw at

JUDGE: The clerk.

BRIGGS: No objections.

O'BRIEN: What's with the detective?

PETROCELLI: He's having problems with a hemorrhoid operation.

BRIGGS: Wait—I didn't know that—maybe we can keep him on the stand for an hour or 2.

CUT TO: CU of PETROCELLI.

PETROCELLI: Detective Karyl, can you describe the scene when you entered the drugstore?

CU: KARYL.

KARYL: It was pretty **gruesome.**

CUT TO: INTERIOR: Camera pans down aisles of neighborhood DRUGSTORE.

CUT TO: MS of JOSÉ DELGADO. He moves in slow motion. He is pale, glancing nervously at a point out of sight of camera. He is explaining something to DETECTIVE KARYL, who stands leaning against counter. The DETECTIVE is heavy, **stooped.**

CUT TO: A shot of open cash register.

....

gruesome horrifying, bloody
stooped bent over

CUT TO: COURTROOM.

PETROCELLI: Are these the pictures you took at that time?

KARYL: The crime-scene photographer took them.

O'BRIEN: May I see them?

MS: PETROCELLI hands pictures to O'BRIEN, who places them before her on desk.

CUT TO: CU of photos. We see legs of the **slain** drugstore owner, NESBITT.

CUT TO: BLACK-AND-WHITE SHOTS from various angles of body in **grotesque** position. Pictures flash in an increasingly **contrasty and grainy format** until they are hardly recognizable.

PETROCELLI: Detective Karyl, when you discovered the body, were there any **signs of life in the victim**?

KARYL: No. But I called the Emergency Medical Service, which is standard procedure.

PETROCELLI: And you noted the open cash register?

....

slain killed, murdered
grotesque ugly, monstrous
contrasty and grainy format unclear and blurry way
signs of life in the victim ways to tell that the victim was alive

KARYL: That's correct. And at that time I asked the clerk was there anything else missing. Often in these cases you might find some cough medicine missing, or some attempt to open a **restricted-drugs case. There's a market for** drugs of any kind.

PETROCELLI: Did you look for other clues, and did you find any?

KARYL: We looked for other clues, but we didn't actually find anything.

PETROCELLI: Eventually you began questioning **suspects** in this case. How did you come across the suspects?

KARYL: We questioned a number of people we felt might have some knowledge of the crime. Then we received **a tip** from a person who claimed he knew what happened to the cigarettes.

PETROCELLI: That would be Mr. Zinzi?

KARYL: That's correct. He told us about Mr. Bolden. Then Mr. Bolden told us about Mr. Evans and Mr. King.

....

restricted-drugs case locked container of medicine
There's a market for A lot of people will buy
suspects people that may have been involved
a tip information

PETROCELLI: And both Zinzi and Bolden had their own motives in doing this?

KARYL: We often use information from **informants**, especially in murder cases.

PETROCELLI: And did you talk to Mr. King?

KARYL: To Mr. King and to some of his associates.

FADE OUT.

FADE IN: INTERIOR: 28TH PRECINCT. STEVE is sitting on a long, dark bench. He is dressed in cutoffs, sneakers, and a T-shirt. There is a basketball on the floor near him. DETECTIVE KARYL is sitting across from STEVE. He is eating a cheeseburger. Sometimes he talks with his mouth full. A Black detective, ARTHUR WILLIAMS, sits on the edge of the table. He is dressed much as STEVE is and looks only a few years older.

KARYL: They're saying that you **pulled the trigger.** King said the **score** was over but you turned back and shot Nesbitt. Why did you do that? I can't figure it.

STEVE: I don't know what you're talking about, man. I didn't do any **stickup.**

....

informants people who tell us information about other people
pulled the trigger shot the gun; fired the gun
score robbery
stickup robbery with a gun

KARYL: You figured you didn't want to leave any witnesses, I guess.

WILLIAMS: What are we **playing with** this guy for? We don't need him. We got the case locked.

KARYL: The DA is thinking death penalty.

WILLIAMS: Death penalty? Chances are the judge will **push for life without parole**. And if they **come clean**, he might even go for 25 to life. You save a lot of time and money that way.

KARYL: I don't know. The victim was well respected in the neighborhood. Hardworking Black guy, worked his way up. He even sponsored a Little League team. The judge could go for the death penalty if they plead not guilty.

WILLIAMS: This guy's only 16. They won't kill him.

KARYL: What are you, a **pessimist**? Hope for the best.

....

playing with questioning
push for life without parole try to send them to jail forever
come clean admit they did it; tell the truth
pessimist person who thinks negatively

CUT TO: Weird shot of INTERIOR: DEATH ROW. STEVE is seen walking down the hallway between two guards. He is brought into the **death chamber**. The guards are pale, almost greenish. They lay STEVE on the table for the **lethal injection and strap him down**.

CU of STEVE's face. He is terrified.

CUT TO: INTERIOR: COURTROOM. KARYL is still on stand as BRIGGS cross-examines.

BRIGGS: Did you dust the area for fingerprints?

KARYL: It's my understanding that the crime-scene technicians didn't find any fingerprints they could establish as belonging to a perpetrator.

BRIGGS: Isn't it true that what you did in this case was to skip the investigation and run to your **stoolies**?

KARYL: We treat each case carefully. We don't just go through the motions.

BRIGGS: The cash register was handled, but you didn't find fingerprints, is that right?

....

death chamber room where people are put to death

lethal injection and strap him down needle filled with poison and tie him down so he cannot move

stoolies criminals who provide information to get less jail time

KARYL: Not clear prints.

BRIGGS: How about the counter—was that dusted for fingerprints?

KARYL: Nothing clear enough to use.

BRIGGS: And it really isn't that hard to find people who are in jail or whom you arrest to swear that somebody else is a bad guy? Isn't that right?

KARYL: We check every story. **We give everybody the benefit of the doubt.**

BRIGGS: But you don't check fingerprints?

KARYL: We check them when we find them.

BRIGGS: Right. Nothing further.

....

We give everybody the benefit of the doubt. We believe every informant is telling the truth until we prove they are lying.

BEFORE YOU MOVE ON...

1. **Inference** On page 53 Steve says he does not feel like he is involved in his own trial. Why?

2. **Conclusions** Why does Briggs object to the way Detective Karyl gets witnesses to give information?

LOOK AHEAD Will Steve have a chance for a fair trial? Read pages 65–73 to find out.

CUT TO: INTERIOR: JAIL. An OLDER PRISONER sits on the john, his pants around his ankles.

OLDER PRISONER: They got to **give you some time**. A guy dies and you get time. That's the deal. Why the hell should you **walk**? And don't **give me young**. Young don't count when a guy dies. Why should you walk?

STEVE: 'Cause I'm a human being. I want a life, too! What's wrong with that?

OLDER PRISONER: Nothing. But there's rules you got to follow. You do the crime, you **do the time**. You act like garbage, they treat you like garbage.

PRISONER 2: Yo, man. You acting like you a preacher or something—but guess where you at? This ain't no hotel.

OLDER PRISONER: But I ain't complaining.

PRISONER 2: But suppose he innocent?

OLDER PRISONER: You innocent?

STEVE: Yes.

....

give you some time sentence you to time in jail
walk be set free
give me young use the excuse that you are young
do the time spend time in jail; pay the penalty

OLDER PRISONER: Yeah, well, somebody got to do some time. They're going to lock somebody up.

PRISONER 3: How's he gonna say he's innocent? That's why they holding the trial—so the jury can say if he's innocent or not. What he says now don't even count.

OLDER PRISONER: Whatever. Anyone got a newspaper?

FADE OUT.

FADE IN: INTERIOR: WAITING ROOM. O'BRIEN enters and sits on bench with STEVE. STEVE's wrist is handcuffed to bench.

O'BRIEN (**indicating** cuffs): This wasn't necessary.

STEVE: They just like to show they're **in charge**. How do you think the trial is going?

O'BRIEN: It could be going better.

STEVE (surprised): What's wrong?

O'BRIEN: Well, **frankly**, nothing is happening that speaks to your being innocent. Half of those jurors, no matter what they said when

....

indicating pointing to the
in charge the boss; in control of me
frankly honestly

we questioned them when we picked the jury, believed you were guilty the moment they laid eyes on you. You're young, you're Black, and you're on trial. What else do they need to know?

STEVE: I thought you're supposed to be innocent until you're proven guilty?

O'BRIEN: That's true, but in reality it depends on how the jury sees the case. If they see it as a **contest** between the defense and the prosecution as to who's lying, they'll **vote for** the prosecution. The prosecutor walks around looking very important. No one is accusing her of being a bad person. They're accusing you of being a monster. The jury can ask itself, Why should the prosecutor lie? Our job is to show that she's not lying, but she's simply made a mistake. How are you feeling? Is your stomach still **upset**?

STEVE: A little better.

O'BRIEN: This afternoon we have an important witness scheduled. This Osvaldo Cruz character. What do you know about him?

....

contest choice to make
vote for believe
upset hurting you

CUT TO: EXTERIOR: NEIGHBORHOOD STOOP. Fourteen-year-old
OSVALDO CRUZ is slim, well built. He has a tattoo of a devil's head
on his left forearm and a tattoo of a dagger on the back of his right
hand between the thumb and forefinger. FREDDY ALOU, 16 and
tough, sits **fiddling** with a beeper he is trying to repair. STEVE is
sitting with them.

FREDDY (to STEVE): What school you go to?

OSVALDO: He goes to that faggot school
downtown. All they learn there is how to be
a faggot.

FREDDY: You let him **dis** you like that, man?

OSVALDO: He don't have no choice. He mess
with me and the Diablos will **burn him up**.
Ain't that right, faggot?

STEVE: I can kick your narrow butt any day in
the week.

OSVALDO: Well, here it is, so why don't you
come and kick it?

FREDDY: You better **chill**; he hangs with some
bad dudes.

....

fiddling playing
dis say bad things about
burn him up beat him up
chill relax; calm down

OSVALDO: He don't hang with nobody. He's just **a lame looking for a name.** Ain't that right, Steve? Ain't that right?

STEVE: Why don't you shut up?

OSVALDO: You **ain't got the heart** to be nothing but a lame. Everybody knows that. You might be hanging out with some people, but when **the deal goes down,** you won't be around.

STEVE: Yeah, and you will be, huh?

CUT TO: INTERIOR: COURTROOM. OSVALDO is on the stand.

OSVALDO (softly, timidly): So Bobo said to me if I didn't help him, he'd cut me up.

CUT TO: STEVE writing on pad.

CU: OSVALDO.

OSVALDO: He said he would cut me up and **get my moms,** too. I was, like, really scared of him.

PETROCELLI: Have you ever seen Bobo hurt anyone?

....

a lame looking for a name a loser looking to be popular
ain't got the heart do not have enough courage
the deal goes down the crime is happening
get my moms hurt my mother

OSVALDO: I heard he messed up a dude **in the projects**.

BRIGGS: Objection.

JUDGE: Sustained.

PETROCELLI: Do you know as a matter of fact if Bobo has hurt anyone **in the hood**?

BRIGGS: Objection! Unless the prosecutor is going to pass out glossaries to the jury, I want her to use standard English.

JUDGE: Overruled.

OSVALDO: He told me he did some time for cutting a guy in the projects.

PETROCELLI: Do you know how old Bobo is?

OSVALDO: Twenty-two.

PETROCELLI: And how old are you, Osvaldo?

BRIGGS: Objection! Why are we suddenly **on a first-name basis**?

PETROCELLI: And how old are you, Mr. Cruz?

....

in the projects in the public housing area
Sustained. I will not allow the question to be asked.
in the hood in your neighborhood
on a first-name basis calling the witness by his first name

OSVALDO: Fourteen.

PETROCELLI: You live on 144th Street; is that correct?

OSVALDO: Yeah, across from the school.

PETROCELLI: I'm going to give you a series of names, and you will tell me if you know any of them. James King?

OSVALDO: Yeah, that's him at that table in the blue suit.

PETROCELLI: Let the record indicate that Mr. Cruz has identified Mr. King. Steve Harmon?

OSVALDO: He's the Black guy sitting at the other table.

PETROCELLI: Let the record show that Mr. Cruz has identified Steve Harmon. (Turning back to Osvaldo) All right. Did Mr. Evans, or Bobo, **make a proposition to you**?

BRIGGS: Leading!

PETROCELLI: Your honor, Mr. Cruz **is a juvenile**!

....

Let the record indicate The trial records will show
make a proposition to you ask you to commit a crime
is a juvenile is not an adult; is a child

BRIGGS: **He's hostile?** He's a juvenile. Do you mean to say he's hostile?

PETROCELLI: No, but you are.

JUDGE: That's not necessary, Miss Petrocelli. You haven't established Mr. Cruz as a hostile witness.

PETROCELLI: Mr. Cruz, how real did you think Mr. Evans's—Bobo's—threat was?

OSVALDO: I thought it was the real deal. You know, like I thought he would mess me up.

PETROCELLI: Were you afraid of Mr. King?

BRIGGS: Objection! If she wants to testify instead of the witness, fine. **Swear her in**, but she can't lead the witness like that.

JUDGE: Sustained.

PETROCELLI: Did you participate in this robbery?

OSVALDO: Yes, I did.

PETROCELLI: Why?

....

He's hostile? He does not want to testify?
Swear her in Make her swear to tell the truth and become a witness herself

OSVALDO: Because I was afraid of them. They were all older than me.

PETROCELLI: Who exactly were you afraid of?

OSVALDO: Bobo, James King, and Steve Harmon.

PETROCELLI: And was Bobo the only one who actually threatened you?

BRIGGS: There she goes again!

JUDGE: Where's she going? That's not leading! You think that's leading? Look, I think it's a good time for a break, folks. Maybe we'll all be **a bit more civil** after a good night's sleep.

LS as JURY **files out**. Then the GUARDS come and cuff STEVE and JAMES KING. MS of OSVALDO passing STEVE. The two young men look at each other for a brief instant; then OSVALDO turns away.

FADE TO BLACK.

....

a bit more civil more polite to each other

files out leaves the courtroom

BEFORE YOU MOVE ON...

1. **Paraphrase** O'Brien says, "You're young, you're Black, and you're on trial. What else do they need to know?" What does she mean?

2. **Comparisons** Compare how Osvaldo acts on the streets to how he acts in court. What does this show?

LOOK AHEAD Read pages 74–87 to see what happens when Steve is face to face with King.

Miss O'Brien's saying that things looked bad for me was really **discouraging**. I wonder if the prosecutor knows what Osvaldo is really like. I wonder if she knows what I'm really like, or if she cares.

This morning one of the guys in the next cell expects a verdict. His name is Acie. He was telling everybody that he didn't care what they said about him. He held up a check-cashing place and shot the guard.

"All they can do is put me in jail," he said. "They can't **touch my soul.**"

He said he needed the money and intended to pay it back once **he got on his feet.** He said that God understood and would give him another chance. Then he started crying.

His crying got to me. Miss O'Brien said the judge could sentence me to 25 years to life. If he did, I would have to **serve** at least 21 years and 3 months. I can't imagine being in jail for that long. I wanted to

....

discouraging upsetting
touch my soul hurt my spirit; do anything to who I am inside
he got on his feet he got a job, a place to live, and money
serve stay in jail

cry with the guy.

As I got dressed, I felt sick to my stomach. Mama **leaves** clean shirts and underwear for me. I thought of her in the kitchen ironing the shirts. I think about myself so much, about what's going to happen to me and all, that I don't think about my **folks** that much. I know she loves me, but I wonder what she's thinking.

Mr. Nesbitt. I thought about Mr. Nesbitt and remembered the pictures they showed of him. When they were **passing** them to the jury I didn't look at them, but afterward, when the jury left, Miss O'Brien took them out and put them on the table in front of us. She made notes about them, but I could tell she wanted me to look at them. I looked at them.

Mr. Nesbitt's right foot was **turned out**. His left arm was lifted and bent at the elbow so that his fingers almost touched the side of his head. His eyes weren't completely closed.

Miss O'Brien looked at me—I didn't see her looking at me but I knew she was. Who was Steve Harmon? I wanted to open up my shirt and tell her to

....

leaves always sets out
folks parents
passing showing
turned out twisted; pointing out

look into my heart to see **who I really was,** who the
real Steve Harmon was.

That was what I was thinking, about what was in
my heart and what that made me. I'm just not a bad
person. I know that in my heart I am <u>not</u> a bad person.

Just before I had to go back to the cell block
yesterday, I asked Miss O'Brien about herself. She said
she was born in Queens, New York. She went to Bishop
McDonnell High School, and then St. Joseph's College
in Brooklyn. After that she **worked her way through**
New York University Law School.

"And here I am," she said.

It sounded like a good life even though she said it
like it was nothing special.

In the holding pen, across from where we enter the
courtroom, the guards were talking about their lives.
One wanted to talk about how much money his kid's
teeth were costing to have them fixed. The other
guard didn't have any kids and he wanted to talk
about **how the Yankees were doing.**

....

who I really was what kind of person I was

worked her way through had jobs to help her pay the
tuition at

how the Yankees were doing how many games his
favorite baseball team had won

We didn't start on time because one of the jurors was late.

"The little blonde," the guard who wasn't married said. "Her old man probably had something for her to do before she left the house."

They laughed. It must have been funny.

While we were waiting, they brought King in and handcuffed him near me. I thought of the movie, of what kind of camera angle I would use.

I could smell the different scents of him. He had on aftershave lotion and some kind of grease on his hair. I could **separate the smells**. Please don't speak to me, I prayed.

"They ain't got nothing yet," he said. "Osvaldo don't mean nothing 'cause they let him walk. Anybody can see that."

I didn't answer.

"You thinking about **cutting a deal**?" he asked.

King **curled his lip** and narrowed his eyes. What was he going to do, scare me? All of a sudden he looked

....

separate the smells smell each scent

cutting a deal telling what happened so you get an easier punishment

curled his lip made a mean face

funny. All the times I had looked at him and wanted to be tough like him, and now I saw him sitting in handcuffs and trying to scare me. How could he scare me? I go to bed every night **terrified out of my mind.** I have nightmares whenever I close my eyes. I am afraid to speak to these people in the jail with me. In the courtroom I am afraid of the judge. The guards terrify me. I started laughing because it was funny. They do things to you in jail. You can't scare somebody with a look in here.

A court officer came in and got us. When I went into the courtroom, I saw a group of kids sitting in front. It looked like a junior high school class.

"Once the trial actually begins there will be no talking," the teacher with them said. "This is **part of the American judicial system,** and we have to respect every part of it."

When I looked at the kids in the class, they turned away from me quickly.

....

terrified out of my mind extremely afraid
part of the American judicial system how the law works in America

I sat down and looked straight ahead. It was easy to imagine myself **sitting where they were sitting,** looking at the back of the prisoner.

....

sitting where they were sitting as a student on a school trip to a courtroom

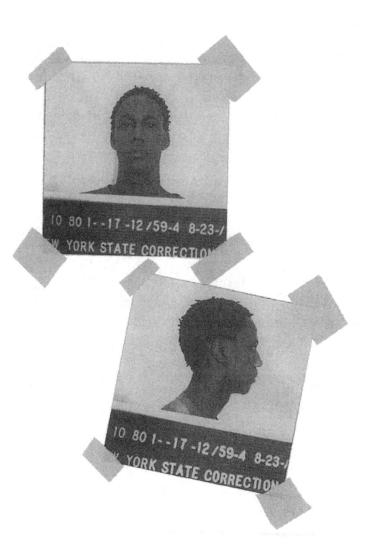

FADE IN: INTERIOR: COURTROOM. MS of JURORS. CU of a PRETTY BLACK JUROR. She is smiling.

CUT TO. CU of STEVE. He smiles.

CUT TO: CU of PRETTY BLACK JUROR. She stops smiling and looks quickly away.

MS of COURTROOM. STEVE has put his head down on the table. O'BRIEN pulls him up.

O'BRIEN: If you give up, **they'll** give up on you. (Then angrily) Get your head up!

STEVE lifts his head. There are tears on his face. As he wipes away the tears, we hear a VO of PETROCELLI as she continues with OSVALDO's testimony.

PETROCELLI: So what did Richard Evans, the man we are **referring to as** Bobo, suggest to you?

OSVALDO: He said he had a place **all lined up**. He said all I had to do was to slow anybody down who came out after them. I was going to push a garbage can in front of them.

CUT TO: PETROCELLI, who appears very confident. Then MS of front of COURTROOM.

....

they'll the jury will
referring to as calling
all lined up picked out; we could rob

PETROCELLI: When Bobo mentioned the other participants, did he **specify what part they were to play** in this robbery?

OSVALDO (getting tougher as he speaks): He said that him and James King were going to go into the store and do the thing. Steve was going to **be the lookout**.

PETROCELLI: And how were the proceeds of this robbery going to be divided?

OSVALDO: Everybody was going to get **a taste**. I don't know how much exactly. But everybody was going to get a taste.

PETROCELLI: And is that taste, or share of the take, the reason you participated in this robbery?

OSVALDO: No, I was in because I was scared of Bobo.

PETROCELLI: Mr. Cruz, you're testifying against people you know. Are you testifying because you're getting a deal from the government?

OSVALDO: Yeah.

....

specify what part they were to play say exactly what each person would do

be the lookout make sure the police or other people were not near the store

a taste some of the money

PETROCELLI: Nothing further.

MS of BRIGGS as he walks slowly to the podium. OSVALDO is obviously an important witness, and BRIGGS treats him like one.

BRIGGS: Mr. Cruz, when you were **apprehended**, did you make a statement to the police about your part in this crime?

OSVALDO: Yeah.

BRIGGS: You admitted to the police that you were a participant in this crime, isn't that true?

OSVALDO: A what?

BRIGGS: You were one of the people involved with the crime?

OSVALDO: Yeah, that's right.

BRIGGS: So **for all practical purposes you were up to your neck** in a crime in which a man was murdered. Is that right? Is that how you saw it?

OSVALDO: I guess so.

....

apprehended arrested, caught
for all practical purposes you were up to your neck the truth
is that you were very involved

BRIGGS: And now that you're in trouble, you'd do pretty much anything to get out of trouble, wouldn't you? And when I say anything, I mean tell lies, get other people in trouble, anything?

OSVALDO: No.

BRIGGS: And when the Assistant District Attorney offered you a deal that would keep you out of jail, you **jumped at it**, didn't you?

OSVALDO: I wouldn't lie in court. I'm telling the truth.

BRIGGS: Well, I'm certainly glad you're telling the truth, Mr. Cruz. But let me ask you, Mr. Cruz, hasn't the prosecutor given you a choice? You go to jail or you put somebody else in jail? Isn't that your choice?

OSVALDO: I don't go around lying to people. Especially **when I swear**.

BRIGGS: And you did swear today, isn't that correct? And it wouldn't be right to lie **under oath**?

OSVALDO: Right.

....

jumped at it quickly agreed to accept the deal
when I swear when I have promised to tell the truth
under oath after you have sworn to tell the truth

BRIGGS: It wouldn't be right to lie under oath, but it would be just fine to go into a drugstore and **stick it up**? That's **cool**, isn't it?

OSVALDO: That was a mistake.

CU of BRIGGS's face showing absolute **disgust**.

BRIGGS: Nothing more.

O'BRIEN stands and takes her place at the podium.

O'BRIEN: Osvaldo, do you know how you were apprehended?

OSVALDO: I had a fight with my girlfriend and she called the police.

O'BRIEN: A fight? You mean an argument? A disagreement?

OSVALDO (quietly): She found out I got another girl pregnant.

O'BRIEN: Are you a member of a gang?

OSVALDO: No.

....

stick it up rob it
cool the right thing to do
disgust hatred, anger

O'BRIEN: So the information I have about you belonging to a gang called the Diablos is wrong?

A beat.

OSVALDO: No, that's right. I belong to the Diablos.

O'BRIEN: So your first answer was a lie?

OSVALDO (Looks toward Petrocelli.): It was a mistake.

O'BRIEN: You also said that the robbery was a mistake. Perhaps you can tell us the difference between a mistake and a lie?

OSVALDO (**ruffled**): Hey, I'm just trying to **turn my life around.** (Looks toward jury.) I made a mistake and now I figure it's about time I did the right thing.

O'BRIEN: How do you get into this gang, Mr. Cruz? Is there something you have to do to become a member?

OSVALDO (getting even tougher): You have

....

A beat. A pause.

ruffled nervous

turn my life around make my life better; change my life and be a better person

to fight a guy who's already in the **club** to show you got the heart.

O'BRIEN: And don't you have to do something else? Something involving a knife?

OSVALDO: You got to leave your mark on somebody.

O'BRIEN: Can you tell the jury exactly what it means to "leave your mark" on somebody?

OSVALDO: You have to cut them where it shows.

O'BRIEN: So to be a member of this gang, the Diablos, you have to fight a gang member and then cut someone. Usually that's done to a stranger, and the cut is made in the face, is that right?

OSVALDO: They don't do that anymore.

O'BRIEN: But Mr. Cruz, that's what you had to do, isn't it?

OSVALDO: Yeah.

O'BRIEN: But now you want us to believe that you participated in this robbery because you were afraid of Bobo, and not because **this is what you do**?

....

club gang
this is what you do you are a criminal

86

OSVALDO: I was afraid.

O'BRIEN: Did you tell the Assistant District Attorney who questioned you that you were a member of the Diablos?

OSVALDO: Yeah, they knew.

O'BRIEN: You weren't afraid to fight a member of the Diablos to get into the gang. You weren't afraid of cutting a stranger in the face. You weren't afraid of beating up your girlfriend. But you were afraid of Bobo, is that right?

OSVALDO: Yeah.

CU of JUROR shaking her head.

BEFORE YOU MOVE ON...

1. **Character's Point of View** Reread pages 77–78. Why does Steve see King in a different way now?

2. **Summarize** How does O'Brien show that Osvaldo could be lying about being afraid?

LOOK AHEAD Read pages 88–98 to see what happens when Steve has a chance to talk to his father.

DISSOLVE TO: INTERIOR: VISITORS' AREA of DETENTION CENTER. There is a table **in the shape of a hexagon**. One side leads to a tunnel through which the PRISONERS can enter. They sit on the inside while the VISITORS sit on the outside. We see STEVE sitting among the prisoners. He is wearing his orange prison **garb**. MR. HARMON, his father, sits on the outside of the table.

MR. HARMON: How are you doing?

STEVE: All right. You talk to Miss O'Brien?

MR. HARMON: She doesn't sound that positive. There's so **much garbage** going through that courtroom, she thinks that anybody in there is going to **have a stink on him**.

STEVE: She said she's going to put me on the stand. Give me a chance to tell my side of the story.

MR. HARMON: That's good. You need to tell them that . . .

His voice fades away.

STEVE: I'm just going to tell them the truth, that I didn't do anything wrong.

....

in the shape of a hexagon with six sides
garb clothes
much garbage many lies and bad people
have a stink on him be judged as guilty

A beat as the father and son try to **cope with the tension**.

STEVE: You believe that, don't you?

CU of MR. HARMON. There are tears in his eyes. The pain in his face is very evident as he struggles with his emotions.

MR. HARMON: When you were first born, I would lie up in the bed thinking about scenes of your life. You playing football. You going off to college. I used to think of you going to Morehouse and doing the same things I did when I was there. I never made the football team, but I thought—I dreamed you would. I even thought about getting mad at you for staying out too late—there you were lying on the bed in those disposable diapers—I wanted the real diapers but your mother insisted on the kind you didn't have to wash, just throw away. I never thought of seeing you—you know—seeing you in a place like this. **It just never came to me** that you'd ever be in any kind of trouble.

MS: STEVE and MR. HARMON. An incredibly difficult moment passes between them. STEVE **searches** his father's face, looking for **the reassurance** he has always seen there.

....

cope with the tension deal with this difficult situation
It just never came to me I just never thought
searches looks at
the reassurance signs of comfort and encouragement

STEVE: How's Mom doing?

MR. HARMON: She's struggling. It's hard on all of us. I know it's hard on you.

STEVE: I'll be okay.

STEVE puts his head down and begins to weep. MR. HARMON turns away, then reaches back and touches STEVE's hand. A GUARD crosses quickly and moves the father's hand away from his son.

MR. HARMON (choking with emotion): Steve. It's going to be all right, son. It's going to be all right. You're going to be home again and it's going to be all right.

The scene blurs and darkens. There is the sound of STEVE's FATHER sobbing.

....

choking with emotion his voice filled with sadness

Notes:

I've never seen my father cry before. He wasn't crying like I thought a man would cry. Everything was just pouring out of him and I hated to see his face. What did I do? What did I do? Anybody can walk into a drugstore and look around. Is that what I'm on trial for? I didn't do nothing! I didn't do nothing! But everybody is just **messed up with the pain**. I didn't fight Mr. Nesbitt. I didn't take any money from him. Seeing my dad cry like that was just so terrible. What was going on between us, me being his son and him being my dad, is **pushed down** and something else is moving up in its place. It's like a man looking down to see his son and seeing a monster instead.

Miss O'Brien said things were going bad for us because she was afraid that the jury wouldn't see a difference between me and all the bad guys taking the stand. I think my dad thinks the same thing.

....

messed up with the pain so sad that I am in jail
pushed down gone, disappearing

FADE IN: EXTERIOR: STEVE's NEIGHBORHOOD. Camera pans. Homeless men have built a cardboard "village" on rooftops. Then: to edge of roof, where we see a crowd in the street below. As camera zooms in, we pick up **a cacophony of sounds**. Gradually one sound becomes clearer. The accent is West Indian, and a ground-level camera comes up on two dark, somewhat heavy and middle-aged WOMEN.

WOMAN 1: I think **it's a shame**, a terrible shame.

WOMAN 2: What happened?

CUT TO: STEVE; he is holding a basketball and is within earshot of the 2 women.

WOMAN 1: They stuck up the drugstore and shot the poor man.

WOMAN 2: Oh, these guns! Is he all right?

WOMAN 1: Miss Trevor say he dead. **They had 2 ambulances.**

WOMAN 2: Two people got shot?

WOMAN 1: I don't think 2 people got shot, but 2 ambulances came. One came from Harlem Hospital.

....

a cacophony of sounds harsh, loud noises

it's a shame it is a terrible situation

They had 2 ambulances. There were two ambulances at the crime scene.

WOMAN 2: It's probably those **crack people**. They say they'll do anything for **that stuff**.

WOMAN 1: Was he married? I didn't see no woman working in the store.

WOMAN 2: That young Spanish boy? I don't think he married.

WOMAN 1: No, girl, he ain't the owner. The old man owned that place. I think he from St. Kitts.

WOMAN 2: Oh, you know it's a shame. You know it is.

LS: STEVE makes his way through crowd. He does not have the basketball. He is walking, then **trots** as the camera **pulls back**. He is running as camera looks from high angle, and we can no longer distinguish STEVE. We hear VO of women as above.

WOMAN 1: I'd move away from here, but there's no place to go. I wouldn't live in California.

WOMAN 2: California is a lot worse than Harlem.

WOMAN 1: But they say the weather is nice.

....

crack people people using drugs
that stuff drugs
trots jogs; runs slowly
pulls back moves away from him

Camera pans down the street, past playing kids and stores to a basketball that lies in the gutter.

CUT TO: Television news; the shot is grainy, the **reception poor** as if it is in the home of a **ghetto** resident.

VO (NEWSCASTER): In New York's Harlem, yet another holdup has ended in a grisly scene of murder. Alguinaldo Nesbitt, a native of St. Kitts, was found shot and killed in his drugstore.

CUT TO: Television shot of front of drugstore. Small children are gathered around trying to get a peek inside.

CU: NEWSCASTER. He is a handsome, light-skinned Black who speaks with a precise television newscaster accent.

NEWSCASTER: Late yesterday afternoon 2 armed and masked **bandits** rushed into this neighborhood drugstore behind me. They first demanded money and, when the store owner, 55-year-old Alguinaldo Nesbitt was slow in handing over the money, viciously ended his life. Residents of the neighborhood are **in absolute dismay.** (To NEIGHBORHOOD RESIDENT) Sir, can you tell me just how shocked you are by this tragedy?

....

reception poor picture hard to see
ghetto poor
bandits criminals, robbers
in absolute dismay feeling very sad and scared

CUT TO: NEIGHBORHOOD RESIDENT.

NEIGHBORHOOD RESIDENT: I ain't shocked. People getting killed and everything and it ain't right but I ain't shocked none. They killed a little girl just about 2 months ago and she was just sitting on **her stoop**.

CUT TO: STEVE's APARTMENT. We see him sitting and watching the news program. We see his brother pick up the remote and change the program. We watch 30 seconds of a *Road Runner* cartoon.

CUT TO: CU of STEVE. He is staring straight ahead, mouth open, in absolute shock as the reflected colors from the cartoon move across his face.

DISSOLVE TO: TWO WEEKS LATER; INTERIOR: STEVE's KITCHEN. Door opens. MRS. HARMON enters with a bag of groceries. She puts it down.

MRS. HARMON: Mrs. Lucas said they **got** those guys that killed the drugstore owner. (She turns on the television.) You have anything to eat?

STEVE: I had some cereal. See if you can **find** the news. You think it's on the news?

....

her stoop the front steps of her house
got arrested, caught
find turn the television to

MRS. HARMON is putting away the groceries when an image of the front of the drugstore appears on the screen. She sits down, obviously pleased that the **culprits** have been caught.

FEMALE NEWSCASTER: An arrest has been made in the robbery and murder in an uptown drugstore. The police announced today the arrest of Richard Evans, known in the community as Bobo. Mayor Rudy Giuliani says that he is determined to stop crime in all areas of the city.

CUT TO: **PRESS CONFERENCE** with MAYOR GIULIANI and **POLICE BRASS**.

MAYOR GIULIANI: The idea that we're just trying to stop crime in white or middle-class areas is nonsense. Everyone living in the city deserves the same protection.

CUT TO: EXTERIOR: MS of a sullen BOBO handcuffed and being led to police van. He glowers at camera. Prisoner he is handcuffed to winks at camera.

CUT TO: INTERIOR: STEVE's BEDROOM. He is lying on his bed, eyes open but not seeing anything. We hear first the doorbell ring and then his mother calling him, but he doesn't react.

....

culprits criminals; guilty people
PRESS CONFERENCE MEETING WITH THE NEWSPAPER AND TELEVISION PEOPLE
POLICE BRASS IMPORTANT POLICE OFFICERS

CUT TO: MRS. HARMON, who wipes her hands on a towel and heads toward door. She stops and looks through peephole. CU on her face. There is a worried look as she opens the door.

MRS. HARMON: (Calls to him.) Steven?

STEVE: Yeah? (He comes out and sees DETECTIVES WILLIAMS and KARYL.)

WILLIAMS: We need you to come down to the **precinct** with us. Just a few questions.

STEVE: Me? About what?

WILLIAMS: Some **clown** said you were involved with that drugstore stickup just before Christmas. You know the one I mean?

STEVE: Yeah, but what do I have to do with it?

WILLIAMS (as they handcuff Steve): You know Bobo Evans?

MRS. HARMON (**mildly panicked**): Why are you handcuffing my son if you just want to ask him a few questions? I don't understand.

WILLIAMS: Ma'am, it's **just routine**. Don't worry about it.

....

precinct police station
clown person we arrested
mildly panicked beginning to worry
just routine just the usual thing we do

MRS. HARMON: What do you mean don't worry about it, when you're handcuffing my son? (There is panic in her eyes as she looks at STEVE, who looks away.) What do you *mean* don't worry about it? I'm coming with you! You're not just **snatching my son off** like he's some kind of criminal. Wait till I get my coat. Just wait a minute! Just wait a minute!

CUT TO: JERRY standing in doorway, holding comics. He looks from MOTHER to STEVE. He reaches out toward his brother as the detectives **hustle** the handcuffed teenager out the door.

CUT TO: MS of STEVE sitting in back of patrol car.

CUT TO: Two OLD MEN in front of John-John's Bar-B-Q looking at the scene as the car drives off.

CUT TO: LS of **block engaged in normal activity**.

THEN: MRS. HARMON rushes from house, looks desperately around, and moves quickly down the street. She gets almost to the corner, then stops, realizing she doesn't know where STEVE is being taken.

....

snatching my son off taking my son away

hustle hurry, rush

block engaged in normal activity people in the neighborhood doing things they do everyday

BEFORE YOU MOVE ON...

1. **Inference** Reread pages 89–91. What is the hardest part for Steve as he watches his father cry?

2. **Symbolism** On page 92, Steve is holding a basketball. What could it mean when his basketball is in the gutter on page 94?

LOOK AHEAD Is Miss O'Brien beginning to trust Steve? Read pages 99–114 to find out.

Miss O'Brien was mad today. She said that Petrocelli was **using a cheap trick**. The judge said he was **calling a half-day session** because he needed to hear pleas in another case. O'Brien said that Petrocelli wanted to leave as bad an image in the mind of the jury as she could. She brought up the photographs again and made sure that the jury saw them a second time. Miss O'Brien said she wanted the jurors to **take the bad images home with them** over the weekend and live with them.

The photos were bad, real bad. I didn't want to think about them or know about them. I didn't look at the jury members when they were looking at the pictures.

I thought about writing about what happened in the drugstore, but I'd rather not have it in my mind. The pictures of Mr. Nesbitt scare me. I think about him lying there knowing he was going to die. I wonder if it

....

using a cheap trick trying to mislead the jury

calling a half-day session ending the trial early

take the bad images home with them think about the horrible photographs at home

hurt much. I can see me at that moment, just when Mr. Nesbitt knew he was going to die, walking down the street trying to **make my mind a blank screen**.

When I got back to the cell and changed my clothes, I had to mop the **corridors** with four other guys. We were all dressed in the orange jumpsuits they give you and the guards made us line up. The water was hot and soapy and had a strong smell of some kind of **disinfectant**. The mops were heavy and it was hot and I didn't like doing it. Then I realized that the five guys doing the mopping must have all looked alike and I suddenly felt as if I couldn't breathe. I tried to suck the air into my lungs, but all I got was the odor of the disinfectant and I started **gagging**.

"You vomit —you just got more to clean up!" the guard said.

I held it in and kept swinging the big mop across the floor. To my right and left the other prisoners were doing the same thing. On the floor there were

....

make my mind a blank screen not think about anything at all
corridors hallways
disinfectant cleaner
gagging to be sick to my stomach

big **arcs** of gray, dirty water and **swirls** of stinking, brown bubbles. I wanted to be away from this place so bad, away from this place, away from this place. I remembered Miss O'Brien saying that it was her job to make me different in the eyes of the jury, different from Bobo and Osvaldo and King. It was me, I thought as I tried not to throw up, that had wanted to be tough like them.

....

arcs curves, patterns
swirls circles, groups

FADE IN: Four-way **SPLIT-SCREEN MONTAGE**: Three images alternate between shots of witnesses and defendants. We hear only 1 witness at a time, but the others are clearly still talking on other screens. In upper left screen is DETECTIVE WILLIAMS. Lower left is ALLEN FORBES, a City Clerk. Lower right is DR. JAMES MOODY, Medical Examiner. The upper right screen is sometimes black, sometimes a stark and startling white. Occasionally the images of those not speaking are replaced with images of KING or STEVE, and we get REACTION SHOTS.

FORBES: It was a registered gun. Our records show that Mr. Nesbitt applied for a license to have a gun **on the premises** in August of 1989. That permit was still **in effect**. The gun was licensed to him from that time.

VO (PETROCELLI): So there was nothing unusual or illegal about the gun being in the drugstore? Is that correct, Mr. Forbes?

FORBES: Presumably he wanted it for the store. That is correct.

SWITCH TO: DETECTIVE WILLIAMS.

WILLIAMS: I arrived at the crime scene at 5:15. There was some merchandise on the floor of the drugstore in between the counters. The

....

SPLIT-SCREEN MONTAGE SCENE THAT LOOKS LIKE SEPARATE TELEVISION SCREENS

on the premises at the drugstore

in effect good, legal

body of the victim was lying halfway . . . his legs were half sticking out from behind the counter. I looked around the counter and observed a middle-aged Black male of approximately 200 pounds. It was pretty clear that he was dead. There was an emergency medical crew there, and they were just **packing it in** when I arrived. I looked around the scene and saw the gun. A uniformed **patrolman** pointed it out to me. I didn't know at the time if it was the gun that killed the victim or not. There wasn't any way to tell without tests. The cash register was open. The change was still in there, but no bills. Also, there were several cartons of cigarettes on the floor, and the clerk mentioned that several cartons of cigarettes were missing. We chalked the body, then had it turned.

VO (PETROCELLI): What do you mean when you say you chalked the body?

WILLIAMS: That's when you put a chalk mark around the **perimeter** of the body to show the position you found it in. We had photos taken, then we chalked the body so we could turn it over and see if there was any possible evidence beneath the victim. I didn't see

....

packing it in putting their equipment away
patrolman policeman
perimeter outside; outer edge

anything there. From the money being gone from the register, I figured it was a stickup and homicide. The guys from the Medical Examiner's office wanted to move the body. It was time for them to get off, and I allowed them to take it.

VO (PETROCELLI): Detective Williams, during the course of your investigation of the crime did you have occasion to speak to a Mr. Zinzi?

WILLIAMS: My partner got a call from this guy on Riker's Island. That was Sal Zinzi. He was doing 6 months on a stolen property charge. There were a few guys in there who were **giving him a hard time**. He wanted out pretty bad. He told me about a guy who had told him about a guy who was selling cigarettes. It **was a slim lead, but we followed it up** until we found a Richard Evans.

VO (PETROCELLI): Known on the street as Bobo?

WILLIAMS: Known on the street as Bobo, right. We **picked him up** and he admitted involvement in the stickup.

SWITCH TO: DR. MOODY.

....

giving him a hard time being very mean to him
was a slim lead, but we followed it up was not a very good clue, but we researched it
picked him up arrested him

MOODY (Nods constantly as he testifies.): The bullet entered the body on the left side and **traversed upward** through the lung. It produced a tearing of the lung and heavy internal bleeding and also went through the **esophagus**. That also produced internal bleeding. The bullet finally lodged in the upper **trapezius area**.

VO (PETROCELLI): And were you able to recover the bullet from that area?

MOODY: Yes, we were.

VO (PETROCELLI): Dr. Moody, can you tell with reasonable certainty the time and cause of death?

MOODY: Death was caused by a combination of **trauma** to the internal organs, which put the victim into a state of shock, as well as by the lungs filling with blood. He wouldn't have been able to breathe.

VO (PETROCELLI): You mean he literally drowned in his own blood?

....

traversed upward moved up
esophagus throat
trapezius area muscles in the back
trauma injury, damage

REACTION SHOT: STEVE **catches his breath sharply**.

REACTION SHOT: KING has head tilted to one side, seemingly without a care.

....

catches his breath sharply breathes in quickly because he is
shocked and upset

Before she left, Miss O'Brien warned me not to write anything in my notebook that I did not want the prosecutor to see.

I asked Miss O'Brien what she was going to do over the weekend, and she gave me a really funny look, and then she told me she was probably going to watch her niece in a **Little League** game.

"I'm sorry," she said. "I didn't mean to **cut you off**."

She smiled at me, and I felt embarrassed that a smile should mean so much. We talked awhile longer and I realized that I did not want her to go. When I asked her how many times she had appeared in court, her mouth **tightened** and she said, "Too many times."

She thinks I am guilty. I know she thinks I am guilty. I can feel it when we sit together on the bench they have assigned for us. She writes down what is being said, and what is being said about me, and she

---

Little League baseball
cut you off interrupt you
tightened looked hard and tight

adds it all up to guilty.

"I'm not guilty," I said to her.

"You should have said, 'I didn't do it,'" she said.

"I didn't do it," I said.

Sunset got his verdict yesterday. Guilty.

"Man, my life is right here," he said. "Right here in jail. I know I did the crime and I got to do the time. It **ain't no big thing.** It ain't no big thing. Most they can **give me is 7 to 10,** which means I **walk** in 5 and a half. I can do that without even thinking on it, man."

It's growing. First I was scared of being hit or raped. That being scared was like a **little ball in the pit of** my stomach. Now that ball is growing when I think about what kind of time I can get. Felony murder is 25 years to life. My whole life will be gone. A guy said that 25 means you have to serve at least 20. I can't stay in prison for 20 years. I just can't!

Everybody in here either talks about sex or hurting somebody or what they're in here for. That's all they

----

ain't no big thing does not matter; is not important
give me is 7 to 10 sentence me to is seven to ten years in jail
walk get out of jail; go on parole
little ball in the pit of little bit of nervousness in

think about and that's **what's on my mind**, too. What did I do? I walked into a drugstore to look for some mints, and then I walked out. What was wrong with that? I didn't kill Mr. Nesbitt.

Sunset said he committed the crime. Isn't that what being guilty is all about? You actually do something? You pick up a gun and you aim it across a small space and pull a trigger? You grab the purse and run screaming down the street? Maybe, even, you buy some baseball cards that you know were stolen?

The guys in the cell played **dirty hearts** in the afternoon and talked, as usual, about their cases. They **weighed** the evidence against them and for them and commented on each other's cases. Some of them sound like lawyers. The guards brought in a guy named Ernie who was caught sticking up a jewelry store. Ernie was small, white, and either Cuban or Italian. I couldn't tell. The police had caught him **in the act**. He had taken the money and the jewelry and

....

what's on my mind all I think about
dirty hearts a card game
weighed thought about
in the act doing the crime

then locked the two employees in the back room with a padlock they used on the front gates.

"But then I couldn't get out because they had a **buzzer** to open the front door," Ernie said. "I didn't know where the buzzer was and I had locked the two dudes who knew up in the back."

He waited for two hours while people came and tried to get into the store before he called the police. He said he wasn't guilty because he hadn't taken anything out of the store. He didn't even have a gun, just his hand in his pocket like he had a gun.

"What they charging you with?" somebody asked.

"Armed robbery, **unlawful detention**, possession of a deadly weapon, assault, and **menacing**."

But he felt he wasn't guilty. He had made a mistake in going into the store, but when the robbery didn't **go down** there was nothing he could do.

"Say you going to rob a guy and he's sitting down," Ernie went on. "You say to him, 'Give me all your money,' and then he stands up and he's like, seven feet

....

buzzer hidden button
unlawful detention keeping people without their permission
menacing threatening to hurt people
go down happen

tall, and you **got to run**. They can't charge you with robbing the dude, right?"

He was trying to convince himself that he wasn't guilty.

There was a fight just before lunch and a guy was stabbed in the eye. The guy who was stabbed was screaming, but that didn't stop the other guy from hitting him more. Violence in here is always happening or just about ready to happen. I think these guys like it —they want it to be normal because that's what they're used to dealing with.

If I got out after 20 years, I'd be 36. Maybe I wouldn't live that long. Maybe I would think about killing myself so I wouldn't have to live that long in here.

Mama came to see me. It's her first time and she tried to explain to me why she hadn't been here before, but she didn't have to. All you had to see were

....

got to run have to run away because he can fight back

the tears running down her face and **the whole story was there.** I wanted to **show strong** for her, to let her know that she didn't have to cry for me.

The visitors' room was crowded, noisy. We tried to speak softly, to create **a kind of privacy with our voices,** but we couldn't hear each other even though we were only 18 inches away from each other, which is the width of the table in the visitors' room. I asked her how Jerry was doing and she said he was doing all right. She was going to bring him tomorrow and I could see him from the window.

"Do you think I should have got a Black lawyer?" she asked. "Some of the people in the neighborhood said I should have contacted a Black lawyer."

I shook my head. It wasn't a matter of race.

She brought me a Bible. The guards had searched it. I wanted to ask if they had found anything in it. **Salvation. Grace, maybe. Compassion.** She had marked off a passage for me and asked me to read it out loud:

....

the whole story was there it was clear how sad she felt

show strong act strong and brave

a kind of privacy with our voices private space between us

Salvation. Grace, maybe. Compassion. A way to be saved from harm. A way to act with kindness.

" The Lord is my strength and my **shield**; my heart trusted in him, and I am helped: therefore my heart greatly **rejoiceth**; and with my song will I praise him."

"It seems like you've been in here so long," she said.

"Some guys have done a whole calendar in here," I said.

She looked at me, puzzled, and then asked what that meant. When I told her that doing a calendar meant spending a year in jail, she turned her head slightly and then turned back to me. The smile that came to her lips was one she **wrenched from some place deep inside of her.**

"No matter what anybody says . . ." she reached across the table to put her hand on mine and then pulled it back, thinking a guard might see her. "No matter what anybody says, I know you're innocent, and I love you very much."

And the conversation was over. She cried. Silently.

....

shield protector

rejoiceth celebrates

wrenched from some place deep inside of her had to work very hard to produce

Her body shook with the sobs.

When she left **I could hardly make it back to the cell area.** "No matter what anybody says . . ."

I lay down across my cot. I could still feel Mama's pain. And I knew she felt that I didn't do anything wrong. It was me who wasn't sure. It was me who lay on the cot wondering if I was **fooling myself.**

....

I could hardly make it back to the cell area I felt so sad that I almost started to cry before I got back to my cell

fooling myself trying to make myself believe that I am innocent

BEFORE YOU MOVE ON...

1. **Connotation** What does Steve mean when he says, "I felt embarrassed that a smile should mean so much" on page 107?

2. **Character's Point of View** Steve's mother believes he is innocent. Why does Steve think he is fooling himself into thinking he is innocent?

LOOK AHEAD Read pages 115–129 to see what Steve and King talk about before the robbery.

CUT TO: EXTERIOR: MS of MARCUS GARVEY PARK in HARLEM. STEVE is sitting on a bench, and JAMES KING sits with him. KING is bleary-eyed and smokes a joint as he talks.

KING: Yeah, well, you know, I found **where the payday is.** You know what I mean?

STEVE: Yeah, I guess.

KING: You guess? What you guessing about when I'm so flat I ain't got enough money to buy a can of beer? I need to put together a payroll crew. Get my pockets fat. F-A-T. I talked to Bobo and he's down, but Bobo liable not to show. When he shows, he shows **correct** but sometime he **act like a spaceman** or something.

STEVE: Bobo's not Einstein.

KING: Whatever. You don't have to be no Einstein to get paid. All you got to have is the heart. You got the heart?

STEVE: For what?

KING: To get paid. I got a sure getover. You know that drugstore **got burned out** that time? They got it all fixed up now. Drugstores always keep some money.

....

where the payday is a place we can rob

correct up on time

act like a spaceman forgets

got burned out that was burned in a fire

STEVE: That's what Bobo said?

KING: Yeah. All we need is a lookout. You know, check the place out . . . make sure ain't no **badges copping some z's in the back**. You down for it?

CUT TO: CU of STEVE looking away.

CUT TO: CU of KING.

KING: So, what it is?

This phrase is repeated as the camera moves farther and farther away, growing louder and louder as STEVE and KING become tiny figures in the **bustling mosaic** of Harlem.

....

badges copping some z's in the back police sleeping in the back of the store

So, what it is? Will you help us rob the drugstore?

bustling mosaic busy scenes

They had scrambled eggs, potatoes, and corned beef hash for breakfast. A lot of guys don't go to breakfast on Sunday, and the ones that do can just about eat as much as they want. The guy behind the **steam table** put a lot of food on my plate and gave me a smile. In here you don't smile back at people who smile at you, so I just walked away.

They had church services and I went. There were only 9 guys in the service, and 2 of them got into a fight. It was a vicious fight and the minister called the guards. They came in and started saying things like **"Break it up"** and "Okay, back off." But they said it in this calm voice as if nothing was really going on and they didn't care if the two guys were fighting or not.

We got **locked down** because of the fight and we were told we had to stay in our cells until 1 o'clock. One o'clock is when the visiting hours start on Sundays.

....

steam table counter of food
"Break it up" "Stop fighting"
locked down locked into our cells

In the cell we played **bid whist** and another fight almost started when one of the guys thought somebody had dissed him.

I think I finally understand why there are so many fights. In here all you have going for you is **the little surface stuff,** how people look at you and what they say. And if that's all you have, then you have to protect that. Maybe that's right.

When we got out, most of the guys **drifted** into the recreation area, and somebody put the television on. There was a baseball game on but it didn't look real. It was guys in uniforms playing games on a deep green field. They were playing baseball as if baseball was important and as if all the world wasn't in jail, watching them from a completely different world. The world I came from, where I had my family around me and friends and kids I went to school with and even teachers, seemed so far away.

I looked down in the street from the corridor leading to the recreation room. Downtown New York

....

bid whist a card game
the little surface stuff what other prisoners think about you
drifted walked

was almost empty on Sundays. The thousands of people who **streamed** through the streets on weekdays were away in their homes. I was looking for Jerry. They didn't allow kids in the visiting area, which was funny. It was funny because if I wasn't locked up, I wouldn't be allowed to come into the visiting room.

At a quarter past one, some women were down in the streets calling up to other women. Then I saw my parents and Jerry.

Jerry was tiny in the street, standing on the corner. The window was **screened** and I knew he couldn't see me, but I raised my hand anyway and waved to him. I wanted to tell Jerry that I loved him. I also wanted to tell him that my heart was not greatly rejoicing, and I was not singing praises.

My parents came, one at a time, and they were both **upbeat** and full of news about the neighborhood and about Jerry.

"Did you see him down in the street?" Mama asked.

---

streamed walked
screened covered with a screen
upbeat cheerful, positive

I told her yes and tried to smile with her. Her eyes were smiling but her voice cracked. In a way I think she was **mourning** me as if I were dead.

....

mourning feeling sad for; grieving for

They left and there was still **too much Sunday left in my life.**

I looked over the movie again. I need it more and more. The movie is more real in so many ways than the life I am leading. No, that's not true. I just desperately wish this was only a movie.

Monday is the State's case. This is what Miss O'Brien said. Monday they bring out their **star** witnesses.

....

too much Sunday left in my life too much of the day left

star best

FADE IN: INTERIOR: COURTROOM. There is a feeling **of expectation in the air**. PETROCELLI, BRIGGS, and O'BRIEN are talking to the JUDGE. PETROCELLI makes a joke and O'BRIEN laughs briefly. They return to their respective tables and the JUDGE nods to the COURT STENOGRAPHER, who **straightens up, ready to take down the day's proceedings**.

PETROCELLI: The State calls Lorelle Henry.

Camera swings to the rear of the COURTROOM. An Assistant District Attorney ushers in LORELLE HENRY. The diminutive 58-year-old retired school librarian is neatly dressed. She was once a beautiful woman and is still quite attractive, looking far younger than her stated age. She moves with grace to the witness stand, avoiding looking at either the jury or the defendants.

PETROCELLI: Mrs. Henry, do you remember an incident that occurred last December in Harlem?

HENRY: Yes, I do.

PETROCELLI: Can you tell us about that incident?

HENRY: My granddaughter **had a cold**. It was just a few days before Christmas and I didn't

....

of expectation in the air that something will happen today

straightens up, ready to take down the day's proceedings sits up, ready to record what people say

had a cold was sick

want it to ruin her Christmas. I had taken her to Harlem Hospital and they said it wasn't serious, but she was still coughing. I went into the drugstore to look for some cough medicine. I was looking over the medicines, trying to figure out which would be best for her, when I heard someone arguing.

PETROCELLI: Do you know what the argument was about?

HENRY: No, I don't.

PETROCELLI: Then what happened?

HENRY: The store owner, Mr. Nesbitt, came over to see what the argument was about, and I heard one of the men who was involved in the argument say to him . . . ask him where the money was.

PETROCELLI: How sure are you that this is what he said?

HENRY (nervously): Not that sure. It's what I think I heard.

PETROCELLI: And what did you see during this time?

HENRY: I saw two young men engaged in an argument. Then I saw one of them grab the drugstore owner by the collar. (She grabs her own collar to demonstrate.)

PETROCELLI: And then what did you do?

HENRY: And then I left the store as quickly as I could. I thought **there might be trouble**.

PETROCELLI: Mrs. Henry, do you recognize anyone present today in this courtroom who was also in the drugstore on the day to which you are referring?

HENRY: The gentleman sitting at that table was one of the men arguing. (She points to KING.)

PETROCELLI: Let the record show that Mrs. Henry has indicated that the defendant, James King, was one of the men she saw in the drugstore on that day. Mrs. Henry, do you remember the day you witnessed the incident at the drugstore?

HENRY: The 22nd of December. It was a Monday. I didn't want Tracy—that's my granddaughter— missing too much school. I thought if she

....

there might be trouble something bad would happen

could get through the next day or so, she would be all right because **of the Christmas break**.

PETROCELLI: Thank you. Nothing further.

CUT TO: BRIGGS at podium.

BRIGGS: Mrs. Henry, did you **have occasion** to see some photographs of Mr. King?

HENRY: Yes, I did. At the police station.

BRIGGS: You heard about the robbery and the death of Mr. Nesbitt and you went to the police; is that correct?

HENRY: That's correct.

BRIGGS: And the police showed you a series of pictures—would you say a thousand pictures?

HENRY: A thousand? No, maybe 30 to 40.

BRIGGS: Maybe 20?

HENRY: I think more than 20.

BRIGGS: Would you say 27?

....

of the Christmas break she would have a chance to rest during her Christmas vacation

have occasion get a chance

HENRY: I couldn't say for sure.

BRIGGS: So the truth is that the police showed you a few photographs and asked you to **cooperate with** them in finding a killer. Is that correct?

HENRY: More or less.

BRIGGS: More or less? Well, I want to get to the truth of this matter, Mrs. Henry. The police did show you the pictures, and they were looking for your cooperation in finding a killer? Is that correct?

HENRY: Yes.

BRIGGS: Mrs. Henry, while you were looking over the pictures, were there **moments of hesitation**? Were there moments when you weren't quite sure, or did you recognize Mr. King as soon as you saw his picture?

HENRY: I didn't recognize him at first, but then I did—the pictures look different than he does in person.

BRIGGS: So how did you recognize him if he looks different in person than he does in

....

cooperate with help, assist
More or less. That is about right.; Yes.
moments of hesitation times when you were unsure

the photographs?

HENRY: I finally recognized him. And when I see him now, I recognize him.

BRIGGS: Mrs. Henry, were you ever given a description of Mr. King? Ever told how much he weighed or how tall he was?

HENRY: No, I was not.

BRIGGS: You said that someone said something about Mr. Nesbitt showing them where the money was, is that correct?

HENRY: That's correct.

BRIGGS: Do you remember who said that? Was it the man you think was Mr. King?

HENRY: I don't know.

BRIGGS: You testified in **a pretrial hearing** that you **had some trouble** testifying that Mr. King was involved in this event, is that correct?

HENRY: I have trouble testifying against a Black man, if that's what you mean.

....

a pretrial hearing an important meeting before the trial
had some trouble did not feel comfortable; did not like

BRIGGS: But somehow you don't have trouble identifying Mr. King at this time; isn't that so?

HENRY: I think I'm doing the right thing. I think I'm identifying the right man.

BRIGGS: Did you ever identify Mr. King **in a lineup**?

HENRY: Yes, I did.

BRIGGS: Was that before or after you saw the photographs?

HENRY: That was after I saw the photographs.

BRIGGS: And how many men were in the lineup?

HENRY: I believe there were 6.

BRIGGS: Six. Only 6. Nothing further.

CUT TO: O'BRIEN sitting at the table. She looks up toward the judge and shakes her head.

O'BRIEN: No questions, Your Honor.

....

in a lineup at the police station when Mr. King was standing in a line of suspects

CUT TO: PETROCELLI.

PETROCELLI: Is there any question in your mind that the man you identified from photographs is the same man who sits at this table?

HENRY: No, there is not.

PETROCELLI: Thank you. Nothing further.

....

Is there any question in your mind Do you have any doubts; Are you at all uncertain

BEFORE YOU MOVE ON...

1. **Inference** On page 116, King asks Steve to be the lookout for the robbery. What could Steve's response mean?

2. **Conclusions** On page 121, Steve says the State will call their star witnesses. Why is Lorelle Henry a star witness?

LOOK AHEAD Read pages 130–149 to see what Bobo wears to court.

MS of BRIGGS, his ASSOCIATE, and JAMES KING.

BRIGGS (to KING): When this guy gets on the stand, I want you to take notes. Just write down any questions you want us to ask him.

KING: Like what?

BRIGGS: Don't worry about it. We just need the jury to know we're challenging this guy.

PETROCELLI: Richard "Bobo" Evans, your honor.

Camera pans to side of COURTROOM, where a COURT OFFICER opens the door and leans out. He holds the door open until RICHARD "BOBO" EVANS enters. He is a big man, heavy, and ugly. His hair is uncombed, and his orange prison jumpsuit is wrinkled.

BRIGGS: Your honor, could we **have a sidebar**?

BRIGGS, O'BRIEN, PETROCELLI and COURT STENOGRAPHER go to side of JUDGE's bench, where they speak in whispers.

BRIGGS: Why is he dressed in a prison uniform? The prosecution is going to try to **connect him to my client**. With him in prison gear, that **prejudices** my client.

PETROCELLI: He refused to put on a suit.

....

have a sidebar meet with you privately

connect him to my client make the jury think that Mr. King and Mr. Evans are friends

prejudices makes the jury form unfair opinions about

We made the offer.

BRIGGS: It's still prejudicial.

JUDGE: To tell you the truth, I don't think it's going to make that much of a difference. This guy looks like a **basket case** and he's going to act like one. I don't want to hold the case up while you convince this guy to wear a suit. Let's get on with the case.

BRIGGS: I'd like to establish the objection.

JUDGE: Okay, and I'll overrule it. Let's get going.

They return to their respective previous positions with PETROCELLI at the podium.

PETROCELLI: Please state your full name.

BOBO: Richard Evans.

PETROCELLI: Mr. Evans, how old are you?

BOBO: Twenty-two.

PETROCELLI: And are you sometimes known by another name? A nickname or tag?

....

basket case crazy person; disturbed person

BOBO: They call me Bobo.

PETROCELLI: Now, Mr. Evans, do you know the people who are seated at these two tables, Mr. Steven Harmon and Mr. James King?

BOBO: Yeah, I know them.

PETROCELLI: How long have you known them?

BOBO: I been knowing King all my life. I just met the other guy before the robbery went down.

PETROCELLI: Before we go any further, Mr. Evans, I notice that you are wearing a prison uniform. **What is your current status?**

BOBO: I'm doing a heavy and a half up at Greenhaven.

PETROCELLI: Will you explain to the jury what a heavy and a half is?

BOBO: Seven and a half to 10 years.

PETROCELLI: And what are you doing the time for?

BOBO: Selling drugs.

....

What is your current status? Why are you in jail now?

PETROCELLI: And you've been arrested before?

BOBO: I been arrested for (Hesitates.) . . . breaking and entering, **grand theft auto**, and one time for taking a car radio and one time for fighting a guy **what** died.

PETROCELLI: So the arrest for fighting a guy that died was **manslaughter**, is that right?

BOBO: Yeah. I got three years.

PETROCELLI: I think the record will show you got 5 to 10 years and served 3. Is that correct?

BOBO: Whatever.

PETROCELLI: Mr. Evans, can you tell me what happened on the 22nd of December of last year?

BOBO: Me and King planned out a getover and we done it.

PETROCELLI: Can you explain to the jury what this particular "getover" was.

BOBO: We **hit** a drugstore.

....

grand theft auto stealing a car
what who
manslaughter unintentional murder
hit robbed

133

PETROCELLI: Can you tell me as much as you can about the plan and about what actually happened?

BOBO: We went over to the place and sat down on a car outside. Then we **got the sign** from him—

PETROCELLI: Let the record show that Mr. Evans is pointing toward Mr. Harmon. Go on.

O'BRIEN: Objection!

JUDGE: Sustained. Is he identifying him or not?

PETROCELLI: Can you identify the man from whom you got the sign that everything was all right?

BOBO: That's him, sitting next to the woman with the red hair.

PETROCELLI: Let the record show that Mr. Evans is identifying Mr. Harmon. Go on.

BOBO: So we got the sign that everything was cool. King took a hit on some crank we had and then we went in. We started **a beef** with

....

got the sign received a signal
a beef an argument; a fight

134

the dude behind the counter. He came up with a chrome and started shouting and stuff.

PETROCELLI: A chrome?

BOBO: Yeah. A gun. Anyway, King was trying to get the gun from him and I was going for the money. Then I heard the gun go off. I looked over and saw the guy falling down and King was holding the chrome. We grabbed what we wanted and **split**. That was it.

PETROCELLI: What else did you grab besides the money?

BOBO: We took some cigarettes and left.

PETROCELLI: Then what did you do?

BOBO: Then we went down to that chicken **joint** over Lenox Avenue, across from the bridge. We got some fried chicken and some wedgies and some sodas.

PETROCELLI: Who was with you at this time?

BOBO: Just me and King.

PETROCELLI: When did you find out that Mr. Nesbitt, the drugstore owner, was dead?

....

split left
joint restaurant

BOBO: The word was in the street that night.

PETROCELLI: What happened to the money you got from the robbery?

BOBO: Like I said, we spent some of it on fried chicken and wedgies. Then me and King **split** the rest.

PETROCELLI: You indicated that Mr. Harmon gave you the all-clear signal so you could proceed with the robbery, is that right?

BOBO: Yeah.

PETROCELLI: And was he to get part of the money?

O'BRIEN: Objection! If Miss Petrocelli wants to testify in—

JUDGE: Sustained! Sustained! Let's **not get carried away**. Rephrase the question.

PETROCELLI: Was anybody else to share in the money?

BOBO: The little Puerto Rican boy was supposed to get a taste and King's friend was supposed to get a taste.

....

The word was in the street People were talking about it
split divided
not get carried away follow the rules

PETROCELLI: You said that you received a sign from Mr. Harmon. Can you tell me what that sign was?

BOBO: He was supposed to tell us if there was anybody in the drugstore. He didn't say nothing so we figured it was all right.

PETROCELLI: And you definitely saw Mr. Harmon coming from the drugstore, as planned?

BOBO: Right.

PETROCELLI: As far as you know, was the shooting of Mr. Nesbitt accidental?

BOBO: I asked King what happened, and he said he had to **light him up** because he was trying to **muscle him**. He was an old man, but he was strong like some of them old West Indian brothers. You know what I mean?

PETROCELLI: Can you tell me how it was that you were arrested?

BOBO (embarrassed): I sold the cigarettes to this guy—his name is Bolden, Golden—something like that. Then he sold some to a white boy and then the white boy **dropped a dime on him**

....

light him up kill him; shoot him with the gun
muscle him fight him
dropped a dime on him notified the police

and he dropped it on me. Once it got going it was 4-1-1, 9-1-1, 7-1-1, I guess they was dropping dimes with 800 numbers, too. Then the cops came and started talking to me. I said I didn't know nothing about it, but then I got **busted on a humble and went down**.

PETROCELLI: Can you explain to the jury how you were busted?

BOBO: Man, this lame-looking brother with an attaché case come up to me and said he wanted to **cop some rocks**. I was so knocked out by this bourgie dude asking for crack that I **slept the real deal. I laid the rocks on him** and he slapped the cuffs on me. Cops don't usually show lame. That was definitely not correct.

JUDGE: He carried an attaché case?

BOBO: Can you believe that crap?

PETROCELLI: Mr. Evans, you were promised a deal for your testimony. Can you tell us what that deal is?

BOBO: If I tell what happened, the truth, then

....

busted on a humble and went down arrested

cop some rocks buy some illegal drugs

slept the real deal did not pay attention

laid the rocks on him gave him the drugs

I can **cop a plea to a lesser charge and pull
10 to 15.**

PETROCELLI: Are you telling the truth today?

BOBO: Yeah.

PETROCELLI: Nothing further.

CUT TO: ASA BRIGGS. He shuffles through some papers, nods
approvingly, and then approaches the podium from which he will
question BOBO.

BRIGGS: Mr. Evans, you admit that you were
in the drugstore, is that correct?

BOBO: Yeah.

BRIGGS: You also admit that you were in the
drugstore to commit a felony. Is that correct?

BOBO: Yeah.

BRIGGS: So you were in the drugstore,
committing a felony—the felony in this case
being robbery—and during the commission of
that felony a man was killed?

BOBO: Yeah.

....

cop a plea to a lesser charge and pull 10 to 15 say I am
guilty of a less serious crime and be sentenced to jail for
ten to fifteen years

BRIGGS: So by your own admission, under New York State law you are guilty of felony murder, for which the possible penalty is 25 years to life without parole?

BOBO: So?

BRIGGS: And you haven't **been tried** for this crime yet. So if you ever want to walk the streets again, you had better find somebody to **take the weight**. Isn't that correct?

BOBO: What you saying? Am I trying to cop a plea? I just told you I was trying to cop.

BRIGGS: And we know who you are, don't we? You're the dope dealer and the thief who could see a man killed and then go over to a fast-food place and have a nice meal. That's who you are, right?

BOBO: I didn't have nothing to eat all day.

BRIGGS: So after you killed Mr. Nesbitt—

BOBO: I didn't kill him.

BRIGGS: As far as this jury knows, you are the only man who admits being in the

....

been tried had a court trial
take the weight take the blame

drugstore when Mr. Nesbitt was killed. You admitted to planning the robbery. You also admitted to taking the cigarettes, and you admitted to being there when Mr. Nesbitt was lying on the floor of the store he had worked so hard for. But now you blame somebody else for the killing to get a break for yourself, isn't that right?

BOBO: I think King was high or he wouldn't have shot the dude. He didn't have to shoot him. He's the cause of me **being in this mess**.

BRIGGS: Not you? You didn't want to do the stickup?

BOBO: Man, later for you.

BRIGGS: Nothing further.

JUDGE: Miss O'Brien?

O'BRIEN (from her chair): Mr. Evans, when did you have a conversation with Mr. Harmon about this robbery?

PETROCELLI (smiling): Perhaps counsel wants to approach the podium?

....

being in this mess being arrested for murder
Man, later for you. I am not talking to you anymore.

O'BRIEN stands and goes slowly to the podium, looking at her notes.

BOBO: I didn't have a conversation with him. He's King's friend.

O'BRIEN: So let me get this straight. What was Mr. Harmon supposed to do if there were cops in the drugstore?

BOBO: Give us a signal.

O'BRIEN: And what was that signal to be?

BOBO: Something to let us know there were cops in there.

O'BRIEN: And if there were no cops in there, what was he supposed to do?

BOBO: I don't know.

O'BRIEN: You said you planned the robbery with Mr. King. Didn't he tell you?

BOBO: I thought King had **it hooked up**. He told me he had everything straight.

O'BRIEN: You testified that you did not have a

....

it hooked up everything planned out

gun when you entered the drugstore. Is that correct?

BOBO: Right.

O'BRIEN: How did you know—how do you know now—that the gun that was used was not brought into the drugstore by whoever it was you were with?

BOBO: King said he didn't have no gun.

O'BRIEN: So you're **relying pretty much on** what you've been told about this robbery. Is that correct?

BOBO: **'Cept what I seen.**

O'BRIEN: And what you saw was when you were actually involved in the holdup?

BOBO: That's right.

O'BRIEN: Did you ever talk to Osvaldo?

BOBO: I said a few words to him.

O'BRIEN: You told him that he had better participate in the crime or you would hurt him?

·····

relying pretty much on trusting, believing
'Cept what I seen. Except what I saw.

BOBO: He wanted in.

O'BRIEN: But he testified that the only reason he was involved in this stickup was that he was afraid of you.

BOBO: I wouldn't bring anybody into a serious **jam** unless they wanted to be there. You can't rely on nobody that don't want to be there.

O'BRIEN: When you were in the drugstore—and you have admitted being there—did you see anyone else in the store?

BOBO: I didn't see the lady.

O'BRIEN: But you know now that a lady was in the store. Is that correct?

BOBO: Yeah.

O'BRIEN: How did you find that out, from Mr. King?

BOBO: Detective told me.

O'BRIEN: King told you about the plans, or what he wanted you to know of them. The police told you about the witness. Are you sure you were there?

....

He wanted in. He wanted to be a part of the robbery.
jam crime

BOBO: I told you I was there.

O'BRIEN: As a matter of fact, your deal depends on your admitting you were there, doesn't it, Mr. Evans?

BOBO: Yeah.

O'BRIEN: Did you talk to Osvaldo after the stickup?

BOBO: No.

O'BRIEN: Did you talk to Mr. Harmon?

BOBO: No.

O'BRIEN: How about the money? Weren't you supposed to split the money up?

BOBO: When we found out the guy was dead, we decided to **lay low**.

O'BRIEN: Who is the "we" who decided to lay low?

BOBO: Me and King.

O'BRIEN: Thank you; nothing further.

....

lay low hide

CUT TO: PETROCELLI, adjusting her glasses.

PETROCELLI: Prior to the robbery, just before the robbery, what were you and Mr. King doing?

BOBO: Just before we went in?

PETROCELLI: Yes, just before you went in, what were you doing?

BOBO: Waiting for him to come out.

PETROCELLI: Who are you referring to when you say "him"?

BOBO: Him, that guy sitting over there.

PETROCELLI: Let the record show that Mr. Evans is referring to Steve Harmon. Nothing further.

O'BRIEN: (Stands quickly.) But you had not spoken to Mr. Harmon prior to the stickup?

BOBO: Naw.

O'BRIEN: And you didn't speak to him after the stickup or split any money with him?

BOBO: I told you we decided to lay low. We

....

Naw. No.

would have given him his cut later when **things cooled down.**

O'BRIEN: Did that time ever come?

BOBO: I don't know what King did.

O'BRIEN: But as far as you know, there was no money given to Mr. Harmon.

BOBO: I don't know what King done.

O'BRIEN: Nothing further.

CUT TO: MS of JURORS from STEVE's point of view (POV). One JUROR, a middle-aged man, looks directly toward the camera for a long time. The camera then moves away as if STEVE has turned away from the accusing stare.

PETROCELLI: The people rest.

FADE OUT.

FADE IN: **Concentric colorful circles** and **hurdy-gurdy music**: A hustling, bustling CARTOON CITY comes alive on the screen. Then a small CARTOON MAN, dressed in an old-fashioned nightgown, looks out of his window.

CARTOON MAN (shouting): The people rest!

....

things cooled down the police went away

Concentric colorful circles Colorful circles that are all linked together

hurdy-gurdy music loud music

On-screen all CARTOON CHARACTERS stop, cars screech to a stop, and then everybody sleeps. The people are resting.

CUT TO: INTERIOR: COURTROOM.

JUDGE: I'll take motions this afternoon after lunch. The defense can start its case the first thing in the morning. It's a nice day out, and we'll adjourn and give the jury the rest of the day off unless somebody has an objection.

We see the JURY leave, then the **various parties leave in turn**. We see MRS. HARMON come over and talk to O'BRIEN. STEVE's MOTHER is **disturbed** as a COURT OFFICER comes over and stands near STEVE.

FADE OUT.

....

various parties leave in turn rest of the people leave also
disturbed upset

BEFORE YOU MOVE ON...

1. **Character** Bobo comes to court wearing his prison clothes and looking very messy. What does this say about Bobo?

2. **Inference** Bobo hardly knows Steve. He says that he never spoke to Steve when planning the robbery. How could this affect Steve's trial?

LOOK AHEAD Read pages 150–162 to find out if Bobo's testimony helped Steve or not.

Tuesday, July 14th

Miss O'Brien came to see me this afternoon. She looked tired. She said that Bobo's testimony hurt us a lot and that she had to find a way to **separate me from King,** but King's lawyer wanted to make sure the jury connected us because I looked like a pretty **decent** guy. She talked to me for almost an hour. Several times she patted me on the hand. I asked her if that meant that she thought we were going to lose the case. She said no, but I don't believe her.

I am so scared. My heart is beating like crazy and I am having trouble breathing. The trouble I'm in keeps looking bigger and bigger. I'm overwhelmed by it. It's crushing me.

It is a nice day on the outside. On the street below, people walk in what looks like a crisscross pattern across the narrow streets. There are yellow cabs **inching along.** On the corner there is a cart that sells food, frankfurters or sausages I guess, and sodas. People stand around buying what they want, then move

separate me from King make the jury know I was not friends with King, and that I was not the same kind of person as King

decent good

inching along driving slowly down the street

away. It looks like something I would like to do, move away from where I am.

Tomorrow we **start our case**, and I don't see what we are going to do. I hear myself thinking like all the other prisoners here, trying to convince myself that everything will be all right, that the jury can't find me guilty because of this reason or that reason. We lie to ourselves here. Maybe we are here because we lie to ourselves.

Lying on my cot, I think of everything that has happened over the last year. There was nothing **extraordinary** in my life. No bolt of lightning came out of the sky. I didn't say a magic word and turn into somebody different. But here I am, **maybe on the verge of losing** my life, or the life I used to have. I can understand why they take your shoelaces and belt from you when you're in jail.

Miss O'Brien made me write down all the people in my life who I love and who love me. Then I had to write down the people who I admire. I wrote down Mr. Sawicki's name twice.

....

start our case try to convince the jury that I am not guilty
extraordinary out of the ordinary; extra special
maybe on the verge of losing about to lose

Mr. Briggs will present King's defense first. Miss O'Brien will go second, but she says she has to be careful because if she says anything that makes King look bad and Mr. Briggs **attacks her**, it will look bad for me.

"We can use some friends," she said.

When she left and I had to go back to the cell area, I was more depressed than I have been since I've been here. I wish Jerry were here. Not in jail, but somehow with me. What would I say to him? Think about **all the tomorrows of your life**. Yes, that's what I would say. Think about all the tomorrows of your life.

When the lights went out, I think I heard someone crying in the darkness.

....

attacks her argues with Miss O'Brien
all the tomorrows of your life your future

FADE IN: INTERIOR: COURTROOM: DOROTHY MOORE is on the stand. She is a brown-skinned, fairly pleasant-looking woman. She looks **sincerely** at ASA BRIGGS.

BRIGGS: And what time do you remember Mr. King coming to your home that afternoon?

MOORE: Three thirty.

BRIGGS: And you're sure of the time?

MOORE (confidently): I am quite sure, sir.

BRIGGS: Nothing more.

PETROCELLI: Mrs. Moore, how often does Mr. King come to your house?

MOORE: About twice a month. He's my cousin.

PETROCELLI: Do you remember the purpose of the visit?

MOORE: He was just **dropping by**. He saw a lamp that he thought I might like and he brought it by. We talked about Christmas coming up.

PETROCELLI: He bought the lamp for you?

MOORE: Yes, he did.

....

sincerely honestly, lovingly
dropping by visiting

PETROCELLI: Do you remember if he was working at the time? Did he have a job?

MOORE: I don't think so.

PETROCELLI: And still he **took** his money to buy you a lamp. You remember how much the lamp cost?

MOORE: No, I don't.

PETROCELLI: But that was nice of him, wasn't it?

MOORE (subdued): I think it was.

PETROCELLI: And you like him a lot, don't you?

MOORE: I wouldn't lie for him, if that's what you're saying.

PETROCELLI: Before this visit, when did you last see Mr. King?

MOORE: I guess a few weeks before that. I don't know the exact date.

PETROCELLI: What kind of work was he looking for?

....

took used

MOORE: Just a job. I don't know.

PETROCELLI: Does he have a driver's license?

MOORE: I don't know.

PETROCELLI: You really don't know a lot about your cousin, do you?

MOORE: I know I saw him that day.

PETROCELLI (condescendingly): And what do you do for a living?

MOORE: I do day's work, but I wasn't working that week, because I had hurt my ankle. I went to the doctor that Monday, and you can check that.

PETROCELLI: You don't have to **verify** what you were doing, Mrs. Moore. Did anybody see Mr. King at your home on that day?

MOORE: I don't think so.

PETROCELLI: Do you still have the lamp? The lamp Mr. King so kindly bought for you?

MOORE: It broke.

....

condescendingly a little disrespectfully
I do day's work I usually work during the day
verify prove

PETROCELLI: **Should I take that to** mean you no longer have the lamp?

MOORE: They don't make things **to last anymore**. I think it was made in Korea or someplace like that.

PETROCELLI: Again, should I take that to mean that you no longer have the lamp?

MOORE: I don't have it now, but I did have it.

PETROCELLI: Yes, of course. Thank you. Nothing further.

CUT TO: GEORGE NIPPING on stand. He is about 50 and wears wire-rimmed glasses. He speaks precisely and generally makes **a good impression**.

BRIGGS: Mr. Nipping, do you know, as a matter of fact, if Mr. King is right-handed or left-handed?

NIPPING: He's left-handed. I know that because when he was a kid, I went out and bought him a glove, a baseball glove, and I had to take it back because he was left-handed.

BRIGGS: Have you ever known him to do

....

Should I take that to Because the lamp was broken, does that

to last anymore very well anymore

a good impression people feel they can trust him

anything **of significance** with his right hand?

NIPPING: No, I've never seen him use his right hand for anything.

We see STEVE writing on a pad.

CUT TO: The pad. O'BRIEN is writing a note under STEVE's question, which reads "**What's that about?**" She writes: "The wound was on the left side of the body, which might mean that the shooter was right-handed. **It's a weak argument.**"

BRIGGS: And for the record, how long have you known Mr. King?

NIPPING: I'd say about 17 to 18 years.

BRIGGS: Thank you.

CUT TO: NIPPING on stand facing PETROCELLI.

PETROCELLI: Have you ever seen Mr. King shoot a man?

NIPPING: No, I haven't.

PETROCELLI: So when he shoots a gun, you don't know what hand he uses. Is that right?

BRIGGS: Objection!

....

of significance special, important
What's that about? Why is it important that King is left-handed?
It's a weak argument. It will not help King's case.

PETROCELLI (ignoring objection): If Mr. King was **struggling** with someone and the gun happened to be on the right side, do you know what he would do?

NIPPING: No, I don't.

PETROCELLI: Nothing further.

CUT TO: FILM CLASS. MS of MR. SAWICKI.

SAWICKI: There are a lot of things you can do with film, but you don't have **an unlimited access** to your audience. In other words, keep it simple. You tell the story; you don't look for the camera technician to tell the story for you. When you see a filmmaker getting too fancy, you can bet he's worried either about his story or about his ability to tell it.

CUT TO: INTERIOR: ROOM where lawyers meet with their clients. SPLIT SCREEN: One side is O'BRIEN, **pacing** nervously. On the other side is STEVE, sitting.

O'BRIEN: You're going to have to take the stand—look at the jury and let the jury look at you—and say that you're innocent. I know the judge will tell the jury not to **infer anything** if you don't take the stand, but I

....

struggling fighting
an unlimited access the ability to tell everything
pacing walking
infer anything make any judgments about you

158

believe that the jury wants to hear from you. I think they want to hear your side of the story. Can you handle it?

We see STEVE nodding **in the affirmative**.

O'BRIEN: The prosecutor's strongest point against you is the connection between you and King. She has Bobo admitting to being in on the robbery and his link to King. You've told me you know King. I don't know why you've chosen this man as **an acquaintance**, but it's going to hurt you **big-time** if you don't manage to get some distance between you and him in the eyes of the jury. You're going to have to break the link. He's sitting there looking surly. Maybe he thinks he's tough; I don't know. I do know you'd better put some distance between yourself and whatever being a tough guy represents.

You need to present yourself as someone the jurors can believe in. Briggs isn't going to put King on the stand. That helps you, but when he sees us separating you from him, he's going to realize that his client is in trouble.

....

in the affirmative that he will be able to handle it
an acquaintance a person to know; a friend
big-time greatly

STEVE: How do you know he won't testify?

O'BRIEN: King made a statement to the police when he was arrested. He said he didn't know Bobo. But the prosecution can prove that's a lie. So if he takes the stand, they can use his own statements against him and **he's cooked.** If you don't testify, you'll just make the tie between you and King stronger in the mind of the jury. I think you have to testify. And the way you spend the rest of your youth might well depend on how much the jury believes you.

STEVE: That woman said that King was with her.

O'BRIEN: Right, but Petrocelli didn't even bother with a lengthy cross-examination. Did you notice that? She **dismissed** Mrs. Moore with her tone of voice. A cousin who likes him testifies that he was with her. Big deal. Against all the evidence against him, it doesn't count for very much. His lawyer is going to rely on **his closing argument** to win the case, and I don't think that's going to be effective unless he's very, very lucky. Cases are won on closing arguments only on television, not in a real courtroom.

....

he's cooked he will lose his case

dismissed rejected the testimony of

his closing argument the speech he gives the jury at the end
of the trial

SINGLE MS: We see STEVE nodding, but he is looking down. We see O'BRIEN looking at him, studying him closely. She sits down and takes a deep breath.

O'BRIEN: (Puts a paper cup on the table.) Okay, Steve, now **stay with me**. We're going to play a little game. I'm going to take this cup and place it on the table. Then I'm going to ask you some questions. When I like the answers you give me, I'll leave the cup facing up. When I don't like the answers, I'll turn it upside down. You figure out what's wrong with the answer you gave me. All right?

STEVE: Why? (O'BRIEN doesn't answer. Then we see STEVE nod his **assent**.)

O'BRIEN: Did you know James King?

STEVE: No?

CUT TO: O'BRIEN turns the cup down.

STEVE: Yeah, **casually**.

CUT TO: O'BRIEN turns the cup up.

O'BRIEN: When was the last time you spoke to him before the robbery?

....

stay with me try to understand what I am doing
assent agreement
casually a little but not very well

STEVE: Last summer?

CUT TO: O'BRIEN turns the cup down.

STEVE: I don't know for sure. I mean, he's not like a guy I talk with a lot.

CUT TO: O'BRIEN turns the cup up.

THEN: The camera moves farther and farther away from **the pair**. We see another prisoner and lawyer enter the room. We don't hear O'BRIEN's questions or STEVE's answers but we see O'BRIEN turning the cup.

FADE TO BLACK.

FADE IN: INTERIOR: CELL at nighttime: We barely see the outlines of the inmates, 2 of whom are sleeping on the floor.

....

the pair O'Brien and Steve

BEFORE YOU MOVE ON...

1. **Summarize** Reread pages 150–152. Bobo's testimony was not good for Steve. Why not?

2. **Conclusions** How could the testimonies of Moore and Nipping help King?

LOOK AHEAD Read pages 163–175 to find out if Steve will tell the truth in court.

VO (INMATE 1): The prosecutor said I was lying. I wanted to ask her what she expected me to do when telling the truth was going to get me 10 years.

VO (INMATE 2): When they **got you in the system, it ain't time to get all holy**. You in the system, you needs to get out the system.

VO (INMATE 1): What's the truth? Anybody in here knows what the truth is? I don't know what the truth is! Only truth I know is I don't want to be in here with you ugly dudes.

....

got you in the system, it ain't time to get all holy have you in jail and on trial, it is not the time to start telling the truth

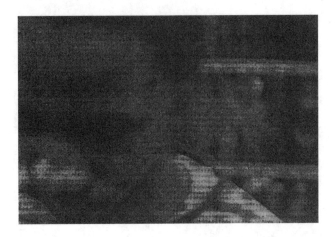

STEVE: Truth is truth. It's what you know to be right.

VO (INMATE 2): **Nah!** Truth is something you gave up when you were out there on the street. Now you **talking survival**. You talking about another chance to breathe some air 5 other guys ain't breathing.

VO (INMATE 1): You get up on the witness stand and the prosecutor talks about looking for truth when they really mean they looking for a way to **stick you under the jail**.

VO (INMATE 3, in a cry for help): I've spent half my life in the joint, man. Where's my life? Where's my damned life?

....

Nah! No way!

talking survival have to do what you can to stay alive and get out of jail

stick you under the jail put you in jail

We hear the toilet flush as scene ends.

CUT TO: INTERIOR: JAIL. STEVE is dressing for court. We see him **checking out** his hand, which is slightly swollen.

CUT TO: STEVE sitting in back of van. He holds his hands out in front of his face. They are shaking.

CUT TO: STEVE on stand.

O'BRIEN: Mr. Harmon, did you act as a lookout for the drugstore robbery or check out the store so that a robbery could be safely committed?

STEVE: No, I did not.

O'BRIEN: Mr. Harmon, did you discuss with anyone that you would act as a lookout or that you would check out the store?

STEVE: No, I did not.

O'BRIEN: Mr. Harmon, were you in the drugstore owned by Mr. Nesbitt, the victim, on the 22nd of December of last year?

STEVE: No, I was not.

....

checking out looking at

O'BRIEN: Are you sure in your mind that you know what a lookout would do?

STEVE: Yes, I am.

O'BRIEN: One last question. Were you in any way involved with the crime that we are discussing here? To make it clear—were you, in any way, involved with the holdup and murder that occurred on the 22nd of December?

STEVE: No, I was not.

O'BRIEN: Nothing further.

CUT TO: PETROCELLI riffling through papers. She stops occasionally, looks toward STEVE, and nods. PETROCELLI leans back in her chair and **visually confronts STEVE for a long beat**. Then she gets up and goes to podium.

PETROCELLI: Mr. Harmon, do you know James King?

STEVE: I know him from the neighborhood.

PETROCELLI: You talk to him much?

STEVE: Once in a while.

....

visually confronts STEVE for a long beat stares angrily at Steve for a long time

PETROCELLI: Once in a while. When was the last time you spoke to him before the robbery?

STEVE: I don't know exactly, but it was during the school year.

PETROCELLI: Didn't you speak to him in December?

STEVE: I don't think so, but I might have.

PETROCELLI: Which is it? You don't think so or you don't remember?

STEVE: Both. I mean, I might have spoken to him, but we don't talk about anything important enough to remember.

PETROCELLI: What do you talk about?

STEVE: Usually I see him in the playground. Maybe he'd say something like "Those guys can't play **ball**," stuff like that.

PETROCELLI: "Those guys can't play ball." Did you ever see him play ball?

STEVE: I don't remember seeing him play ball.

....

ball basketball

PETROCELLI: You having trouble remembering what you've seen?

STEVE: No, but I've seen a lot of ball games. I watch a lot of ball games.

PETROCELLI: Are you nervous? Do you want to **take a few minutes**?

STEVE: No.

PETROCELLI: You talk to Bobo sometimes?

O'BRIEN: Objection. We've been referring to the witness as Mr. Evans.

JUDGE: Sustained.

PETROCELLI: Have you spoken with Mr. Evans?

STEVE: I might have said "Hi" to him. I've never had a conversation with him.

PETROCELLI: You ever talk to Mr. Cruz? Osvaldo Cruz?

STEVE: Yes, he's about my age. I've talked with Osvaldo.

PETROCELLI: What did you talk to Mr. Cruz about?

....

take a few minutes take a break; stop answering questions
for a few minutes

STEVE: Same thing, mostly. About playing ball, or the weather. Or what's going on in the neighborhood.

PETROCELLI: Did you hear Mr. Evans's testimony that—let me put it this way—you heard Mr. Evans's testimony that you came out of the drugstore just before the robbery. Is that right?

STEVE: I heard his testimony.

PETROCELLI: And are you saying it was **just a coincidence** that you were coming out of the store at that time?

CUT TO: FLASHBACK of O'BRIEN turning over the cup.

CUT TO: STEVE on witness stand.

STEVE: I don't know exactly when the robbery happened, but I know I wasn't in the drugstore that day.

PETROCELLI: So Mr. Evans was lying?

STEVE: I don't know what he was doing, but I know I wasn't in the drugstore.

....

just a coincidence just strange timing

PETROCELLI: You heard Mr. Cruz say that you were supposed to go in and "check the store out" for cops. Is that right?

O'BRIEN: Objection! I believe the testimony was that Mr. Cruz was told that was the case.

JUDGE: Do you want the testimony read back?

PETROCELLI: I'll withdraw the question **as framed**. Mr. Harmon, do you remember Osvaldo saying that he understood you to be the lookout?

STEVE: I heard him say that.

PETROCELLI: And according to you, Mr. Cruz was lying, too?

STEVE: No, somebody could have told him that, but I know I wasn't there.

PETROCELLI: Then he must have lied, is that right?

O'BRIEN: Objection. The prosecution is **soliciting an argument**.

PETROCELLI: Withdrawn. Mr. Harmon, you say you weren't at the drugstore anytime during the

----

as framed as worded; as asked

soliciting an argument trying to force the witness to say that other witnesses are lying

day of the robbery. Perhaps you would tell us where you were.

STEVE: I don't know exactly where I was when the robbery took place. Most of the day I was going around **taking mental notes** about places I wanted to film for a school film project.

PETROCELLI: Well, if you don't know exactly where you were, can you tell me anyone who might know where you were?

STEVE: I don't even remember where I was. When the detectives asked me where I was, I couldn't even remember the day they were talking about. They didn't ask me about it until weeks later.

PETROCELLI: Then how do you remember—what did you say?—taking mental notes for a school film project?

STEVE: I know that because I was planning to do the film of my neighborhood over the holidays.

PETROCELLI: Getting back to Mr. King. Would you consider yourself a friend of his or an acquaintance?

....

taking mental notes thinking and memorizing details

STEVE: An acquaintance.

PETROCELLI: Mr. Cruz, friend or acquaintance?

STEVE: Acquaintance.

PETROCELLI: Mr. Bobo Evans, friend or acquaintance?

STEVE: Acquaintance.

PETROCELLI: So you're acquainted with everyone involved in this robbery, is that—

BRIGGS: Objection! **She knows better than that!** She knows better than that!

JUDGE: Sustained. The jury will disregard the last question. There is no one who was involved in this **affair** until the jury makes that decision. And yes, Miss Petrocelli, you do know better.

PETROCELLI (satisfied): Nothing further.

We see STEVE stand shakily and head back to the defense table. He looks out onto the onlookers and sees his parents. His MOTHER forces a smile and his FATHER makes a fist and nods **emphatically**. We see STEVE sit down, start to pick up a glass of

....

She knows better than that! The prosecutor knows she cannot say who was involved in the robbery!

affair crime

emphatically to show he supports Steve

water, and have to put it down because his hand is shaking so badly. O'BRIEN crosses to the desk and writes on the pad in front of STEVE. We see what she has written. It says "TAKE DEEP BREATHS."

O'BRIEN: The defense calls George Sawicki.

CUT TO: CU of GEORGE SAWICKI.

O'BRIEN: Mr. Sawicki, do you know the defendant sitting at this table?

SAWICKI: I've known Steve for three years. He's been in my film club.

O'BRIEN: Can you give us your opinion of Mr. Harmon's work?

SAWICKI: I think he's an outstanding young man. He is talented, bright, and **compassionate**. He's very much involved with **depicting** his neighborhood and environment in a positive manner.

O'BRIEN: Do you consider him an honest young man?

SAWICKI: Absolutely.

....

compassionate always thinks of other people's feelings
depicting showing
Absolutely. Yes.

O'BRIEN: When he says he was taking mental notes for a film, would that be a film for your club?

SAWICKI: Yes.

O'BRIEN: Nothing further.

CU of MR. SAWICKI. He starts to leave the stand but is then held up by the JUDGE.

CUT TO: PETROCELLI.

PETROCELLI: You said you're a teacher in Mr. Harmon's school. Do you live in his neighborhood?

SAWICKI: No, I don't.

PETROCELLI: So although you want to **vouch for his character**, isn't it fair to say that you don't know what he does when he goes to his neighborhood and you go home to yours?

SAWICKI: No, it's not. His film footage shows me what he's seeing and, **to a large extent**, what he's thinking. And what he sees, the **humanity** of it, speaks of a very **deep** character.

....

vouch for his character tell us that Steve is a good person
to a large extent in a big way
humanity kindness
deep strong

PETROCELLI: What was he doing on the afternoon of December 22nd? Did he show you a film of that day?

SAWICKI: No, he did not.

PETROCELLI: Do you feel that the ability to make a film means that someone is honest?

SAWICKI: It is my belief that to make an honest film, **one** has to be an honest person. I would say that. And I do believe in Steve's honesty.

PETROCELLI: As a matter of fact you like him quite a bit, don't you?

SAWICKI: Yes, I do.

PETROCELLI: Nothing further.

O'BRIEN: Harmon rests.

BRIGGS: King rests.

....

one that person

BEFORE YOU MOVE ON...

1. **Character** Reread what Steve wrote in his diary on page 91. His testimony on page 165 seems to be a lie. Why does Steve lie in court?

2. **Paraphrase** On page 175, what does Mr. Sawicki mean when he says that only an honest person can make an honest film?

LOOK AHEAD Read pages 176–196 to see the closing arguments for King's case.

CUT TO: STEVE lying on his cot, soaked with sweat. He tries hard to catch his breath. He turns his head to the wall. He lifts one hand and lets it slide slowly down the pale-green wall.

CUT TO: INTERIOR: COURTROOM: CU of JAMES KING. He looks around awkwardly as BRIGGS **sums up** his defense.

VO (BRIGGS): So what do we have? We have a man who admits to being part of a robbery accusing another man. And why is he making these accusations? The prosecution would have you believe that bringing Mr. Evans, this "Bobo" character, here, is the result of good police work, which gives Mr. Evans the chance to demonstrate what a great citizen he is. But isn't the truth of the matter that the only reason he's here is because the police **have him on a criminal matter**, and have offered him a deal if he comes here and **implicates** someone else? Isn't that the real story?

Does it really surprise anyone that a man who is capable of robbing a drugstore, and he has admitted to doing just that, who then sells the **loot** from the robbery, and he has admitted to that, and who is caught with drugs, and he has admitted to that—then tries to get a lighter sentence by testifying against another

....

sums up finishes
have him on a criminal matter have arrested him for a crime
implicates accuses, blames
loot stolen items

person? Isn't his character, if you can call it character, clear? Hasn't he proven **by his own admissions** who he is? What he is?

Camera pulls back from POV of JUDGE. We see only MR. and MRS. HARMON on one side of COURTROOM, a few strangers on the other side. The COURTROOM is nearly empty. The camera pans to COURT CLERK, who is going through mail. Then to court STENOGRAPHER, who takes down proceedings. Then to COURT OFFICER, who is nodding, close to sleep.

BRIGGS: What I **submit to you**, ladies and gentlemen of the jury, is that Mr. Evans made the mistake of selling the cigarettes he stole during the robbery. Did he do the shooting? I don't know. But naturally he says he didn't do it. If he had sat up there on the witness stand and said he did the shooting, he would never have been offered the deal he got. The only way out for him is to look around and find somebody else to accuse. And that's precisely what he did. He could have picked anyone else in the neighborhood. Half the young men of that age group **are either unemployed or underemployed**. He happened to pick Mr. King.

The State did not produce one witness to

....

by his own admissions from what he said in court

submit to you ask you to think about

are either unemployed or underemployed do not have jobs or are not paid enough

the murder. They produced one witness, Miss Henry, who said she saw Mr. King in the store. **Where was her mind** at the time? According to her testimony, it was on the health and well-being of her grandchild. Could she have made a mistake? Evidently she has. Not that she did not see someone in the store, but whom did she see? She was taken to the police station and given a set of photographs. From these photographs she picked, **at police urging**, Mr. King. But she didn't pick out this photo from a thousand photographs, or a book of photographs or even 50 photographs. She was shown a handful of photos and asked to pick one. Later, when she had to pick someone from a lineup, what was she doing? Was she picking out the man she saw in the drugstore, or was she picking out the man the police had given her in the photographs? That's for you, the jury, to decide. We heard Mrs. Moore testify that James King was at her house at the time of the incident. Shall we assume that every person who is related to an accused person is going to lie? I don't think so. The prosecution, Miss Petrocelli, **paraded in front of you** a bunch of admitted criminals, people who have participated in stickups, buying and

....

Where was her mind What was she thinking about
at police urging because the police told her to
paraded in front of you brought in

selling stolen goods, you name it. She has asked you to believe them. Then she asks you not to believe Mrs. Moore, who has never committed a crime in her life. Think about it. If you met these people on the street, which would you believe, which would you trust?

As for Osvaldo Cruz, he is putting as much distance between himself and this crime as possible. All he was supposed to do was to stand outside and push a garbage can in front of **a potential pursuer**. But there wasn't a pursuer, because Mr. Evans and whoever he was with—if indeed he *was* with anyone else—made sure of that. And think about this: Lorelle Henry, who seemed for all the world like a decent, **law-abiding** human being, testified that she was sure that there were 2 men in the store, 2 men involved in the robbery. And we have 2 men who have admitted participation. I submit to you that there's no need to **go beyond these two** when you look for the perpetrators of this crime. Ultimately, what this case is about is whether you believe people who are admitted participants in this crime and who are saving their own hides. If you believe, as I do, that their positions,

....

a potential pursuer anyone who might chase the robbers

law-abiding honest

go beyond these two look for anyone else involved in the crime other than Mr. Cruz and Mr. Evans their stated characters, **so taint** their testimony that everything they say is **well within the area of reasonable doubt**, then you have no choice but to find Mr. King not guilty. And when you walk away from the sorry testimony of the State's witnesses, you have nothing else from the prosecution. Nothing else. Ladies and gentlemen, at the beginning of this case the prosecutor spoke of monsters. She not only found them, but she has brought them here to testify for the State. I have faith in you, and **faith** in the American judicial system. And that faith leads me to believe that justice in this case **demands** more proof than you have seen in this case. I believe that justice demands that you reject the testimony of these men, consigning their stories to the area of deep doubt. I believe that justice demands that you return a verdict of Not Guilty. Thank you.

CUT TO: POV of JURY. Camera will follow O'BRIEN as she paces from one side of the JURY to the other. Behind her we see the prosecutor's table and the 2 defense tables. Beyond that we see STEVE's MOTHER, sitting on the edge of her seat.

O'BRIEN: First, I would like to thank you for your patience in this trial, and for your

....

so taint hurt, damage
well within the area of reasonable doubt likely to be false
faith belief, trust
demands requires, needs

attentiveness. It's been clear to everyone involved in this case that you have taken an interest in these proceedings and have brought your minds and hearts to the testimony. I would like to **beg your indulgence** while I review that testimony.

The most important testimony, the reason we're here, is the Medical Examiner's statement that a murder was committed. A man is dead. But nowhere in the Medical Examiner's testimony does he indicate who was responsible for that murder. That is for you to determine. It is an **awesome** responsibility. It was testified that the gun belonged to the victim. So we can't **trace gun ownership back to** the murderer. What can we trace as to the guilt or innocence of my client, Steve Harmon?

The State doesn't even suggest that he was in the store during the robbery. It doesn't suggest that it was his gun that was used. The State does contend that somewhere, sometime, Steve got together with someone and agreed to participate in this robbery. On the stand Steve admitted to having seen Mr. Evans on the street in his neighborhood. Hundreds, perhaps even thousands of people have seen

....

attentiveness attention to the details
beg your indulgence ask for your patience
awesome important
trace gun ownership back to use the gun to find

Mr. Evans in the streets of Harlem. Perhaps hundreds of thousands of people. That doesn't make any of them guilty of a crime. The State did **elicit from Steve** that he spoke to Mr. King about basketball. The conversations were short, and **without substance**. At no time did the State establish any conversation between Steve and anyone else about a robbery. Think about that for a minute.

Without a plan that says that Steve **entered an agreement with** the robbers, what would he be charged with? Talking about basketball in the

elicit from Steve get Steve to admit
without substance were not about anything important
entered an agreement with agreed to help

streets of Harlem? Does that now **constitute** a crime? Not in any **law journal** that I know about. The State also presents Mr. Evans's testimony that he "understood" that Steve was to check out the drugstore to see if it was clear. Oh, really? The State brought out a witness, one who everyone agrees has no reason to lie, Lorelle Henry. Miss Henry said that she was in the drugstore when the robbery began. If someone was to make sure that the drugstore was clear, he or she **made a bad job of it**. Remember, it was the State that proved that the drugstore wasn't clear. And do you remember the signal that Mr. Evans said he

....

constitute mean he committed

law journal magazine about the law

made a bad job of it did a bad job as a lookout

received? He said that Steven came out of the drugstore and didn't signal that anything was wrong. In other words, there was no signal. What is the **significance** of this? Well, if there were a signal, a thumbs-up sign, for example, we might expect someone in the **vicinity** to have noticed it. Not only did no one **without a stake** in this case see Steve Harmon giving a sign, Lorelle Henry, a retired librarian, did not see him in the store either. And tell me, how many young black men went into that drugstore that day and walked out without making a signal? Were they all guilty of something?

Do you remember Mr. Evans's testimony that they stopped for a **"quick bite"** after committing the crime? And who stopped for the quick bite? Do you remember? Let me read to you from the testimony of Mr. Bobo Evans. (O'BRIEN picks up notes, adjusts her glasses, and begins to read.)

Mr. Evans: We took some cigarettes and left.

Ms. Petrocelli: Then what did you do?

Mr. Evans: Then we went down to that chicken joint over Lenox Avenue, across from the

....

significance importance
vicinity area
without a stake who did not participate
"quick bite" "fast meal"

bridge. We got some fried chicken and some wedgies and some sodas.

Ms. Petrocelli: Who was with you at this time?

Mr. Evans: Just me and King.

(SHE takes off glasses and looks at jury.) Where was Steve Harmon, the alleged lookout man? Why was there no testimony that Mr. Harmon received part of the loot from this "getover"? The only person we know who profited was Bobo Evans, and we know he made a profit because he sold the cigarettes!

Mr. Briggs has already suggested that the major reason for the testimonies of Mr. Evans and Osvaldo Cruz was **self-interest**. They were brought here not to **answer** for their participation, but for the **sole** purpose of testifying against others. They both understand that the deal they get *depends* on their convincing you that other people are implicated. Mr. Evans suggests that he believed what the "shooter" told him about someone else checking out the store. But let's look at **the reliability of** Mr. Evans's testimony. A robbery was committed; a man was

....

self-interest to protect themselves
answer be punished
sole only, single
the reliability of how much we can believe

brutally killed. The killing here is the key to what these proceedings are about, not the stolen cigarettes, and you understand that. But still Mr. Evans goes around selling the cigarettes that connect him with the crime! Did he think that was a **clever move**? Or is this a **shallow, gullible man** who doesn't think about very much of anything? Who among us can watch a man die in a drugstore and then go out for a quick bite a few blocks away? Is this a man whom we can trust to tell the truth about anything? I don't believe him. Do you?

In going over my notes last night, I **ran into** a question. It's the prosecutor's job to bring all of the participants in a crime to justice, and so Miss Petrocelli has brought everyone she believes might have been involved to this courtroom. But why, if Steven Harmon is innocent, would Mr. Evans want to hurt him? That bothered me quite a bit. But then I thought again about who Mr. Evans was. He had no problem at all in sticking up an innocent man, Mr. Nesbitt. You watched him testify. Did he seem at all bothered by the fact that he had left a man dead? To Mr. Evans, all Mr. Nesbitt represented was a "getover." That's

....

clever move smart thing to do
shallow, gullible man selfish man who is easily fooled and
ran into thought of

what Steve Harmon is to him as well. Mr. Evans—Bobo—is perfectly willing to leave Steven Harmon lying on a floor or **wasting away** in a jail cell. The only thing that Steven Harmon is to Mr. Evans is another "getover."

Finally, let us come to the character of Steve Harmon. (We see O'BRIEN stop and get a drink of water. Then we see her walk next to STEVE.)

I want you to think about his character **as opposed to that** of the witnesses for the State. You saw him on the stand. He answered the questions openly and honestly, as would any other young person of his age. Miss Petrocelli asked him if he was nervous. Do you remember that? The implication was that if he was nervous, it meant that he had something to hide. I submit to you, the jurors in this case, that you, too, would have had a **degree** of nervousness. He's on trial for his life! He's facing the possibility of spending his entire youth behind bars! **Under the circumstances** I would have been shocked if he were not nervous. The State paraded before you witness after witness who, by their own admission, testified either to get out of jail or to prevent themselves from going to jail,

....

wasting away spending the rest of his life

as opposed to that compared to the characters

degree little bit

Under the circumstances Since he is possibly facing life in jail

or, in the case of Mr. Zinzi, to prevent himself from being sexually molested. Think of Steve Harmon's character as opposed to that of Bobo Evans. Compare Steven Harmon to Mr. Zinzi, another of the State's witnesses. Compare him to Mr. Cruz, who admitted taking part in this crime, who admitted that to become a member of his gang, he had to slash a stranger in the face.

Is there reasonable doubt as to Steve Harmon's guilt? I think the doubt was established when Lorelle Henry did not identify Steve as being in the store. It was **reinforced** with every witness the State brought to the stand.

It's up to you, the jury, to find guilt where there is guilt. It is also up to you to acquit when guilt has not been proven. There is no question in my mind that in this case, **as regards** Steve Harmon, guilt has not been proven. I am asking you, on behalf of Steve Harmon, and in the name of justice, to **closely consider** all of the evidence that you have heard during this last week. If you do, I'm sure you'll return a verdict of Not Guilty. And that will be the right thing to do. Thank you.

....

reinforced proven
as regards when speaking of
closely consider think a lot about

MS: PETROCELLI from POV of JURY. Behind her we see the prosecutor's table and the two defense tables. We see the two defense lawyers watching intently. Neither STEVE nor KING is directly facing the camera.

PETROCELLI: I would also like to thank you for your attention in this trial. The defense has just given you its version of the facts in this case, and now it is the State's turn.

Let me start by **refocusing** this case. The defense wants you to go into the jury room thinking that this case is about the character of Mr. Zinzi, who testified that he heard a story about someone who stole cigarettes. It is not about his character. The defense wants you to think that this case is about the character of Mr. Bolden, who bought cigarettes. It is not about his character. The defense wants you to consider the character of Osvaldo Cruz. But this case is not about whether Mr. Cruz is someone we would invite to a party or have as a friend. The defense wants you to **dwell on** the character of Richard "Bobo" Evans. He is not a nice man, they are saying, and so you should **discount** his testimony. But this case is not about the character of any of these witnesses. This case

---

refocusing helping you think another way about

dwell on think about

discount not believe; not consider

is about a crime that was committed on the 22nd of December in which an innocent man, Alguinaldo Nesbitt, was brutally murdered. I don't know what kind of man Mr. Nesbitt was, but I know he did not deserve to be killed in his store, left on the floor while his killers snacked at a fast-food restaurant. This case is not about the characters of Zinzi, Bolden, Cruz, or Evans; it is about Mr. Nesbitt's right to live, and to enjoy **the fruits of his labor.** It is about the right we all have to life, liberty, and the **pursuit of happiness.** It is the **contention** of the State that no one has the right to **deprive us of** the precious gift of life. It is the contention of the State and it is also the law of the land.

A lot has been said about the motivation of some of the witnesses. They testified, according to the defense, only because they were given a break in their sentencing. Therefore, the defense would have you believe, their testimony is somehow made false. Well, let's reexamine their testimony and find out.

CUT TO: CU of JUDGE. He is taking notes.

CUT TO: MS of PETROCELLI from JUDGE's POV.

....

the fruits of his labor the results of his hard work
pursuit of happiness chance to do what makes us happy
contention argument, belief
deprive us of take away from us

Mr. Bolden testified that he received stolen cigarettes from Mr. Evans. We know that the cigarettes were stolen from the drugstore. José Delgado, the drugstore clerk, testified that the cigarettes were stolen. In other words, Mr. Delgado verifies Mr. Bolden's testimony. Did he get a break in sentencing? Or was he simply telling the truth? Did you notice that none of the defense lawyers **questioned** the character of the clerk or even mentioned it? They want you to forget him.

Mr. Evans testified that he was actually in the drugstore, taking an active part in the robbery. No one has questioned that. He also places Mr. King in the drugstore with him on the 22nd of December. This testimony was backed up by Lorelle Henry—Lorelle Henry, who had gone to the drugstore to get medicine for her grandchild. Did she get a break in sentencing? Or was she merely telling the truth? When the defense talks about character, they carefully **skirt around** the character of Lorelle Henry.

Mr. Evans also testified that when he arrived at the scene, he saw Osvaldo Cruz there. This testimony was verified by Mr. Cruz. Yes, I was

---

questioned asked about; were unsure about
skirt around avoided

there, Mr. Cruz testified. Yes, I was part of this robbery. We have three witnesses to the fact that James King was in the store on the 22nd of December: Mr. Evans, Mr. Cruz, and Ms. Henry.

Mr. Evans testified that they did not have a gun but intended to take Mr. Nesbitt's money by **force of muscle**. He said that Mr. Nesbitt produced a gun that he owned. You heard the City Clerk testify that the gun used to kill Mr. Nesbitt was registered to him. Did the City Clerk, who verified Mr. Evans's testimony, get a break in sentencing? Of course not. Did the defense **attack** his character? No, the only thing they could do was to sit and listen to the truth.

Another fact that the defense did not choose to deal with is the sale of cigarettes. The sale of cigarettes to Mr. Bolden, a fact never seriously challenged by the defense, along with the verified theft of cigarettes from the drugstore, also suggests that Mr. King was present in the store during the robbery and murder. Mr. Briggs, the attorney for James King, suggests that Mr. Evans was in the drugstore by himself, or perhaps with Osvaldo

....

force of muscle using their strength and beating him up if they had to

attack ask questions about

Cruz. But Lorelle Henry identified Mr. King as the man she saw in the drugstore. Here is a Black woman, **uneasy about her role in** identifying a young Black man, who still had the courage to testify before you and to positively identify Mr. King. Mr. Briggs's **theory simply does not work**. What does work is the State's theory of what happened, verified by all of the witnesses. Mr. Harmon gave the all-clear signal, and Bobo Evans and James King went into the store to rob Mr. Nesbitt. When Mr. Nesbitt tried to defend himself, the gun was taken from him and he was shot by that man, sitting right there (She points to King.), and killed. Ms. O'Brien suggests that if Mr. Harmon had actually **cased** the drugstore for the robbers, he would have seen Ms. Henry. In other words, he would have been a better lookout man. Well, maybe he hasn't had much experience in helping to rob drugstores. Should we feel sorry for him? For that matter, are Mr. King or Mr. Evans so accomplished in their criminal activities? This was a **botched** robbery in which the perpetrators actually took very little money and a few cartons of cigarettes. And, oh, yes, the life of a good man, Alguinaldo Nesbitt.

---

uneasy about her role in uncomfortable about
theory simply does not work story is not possible
cased acted as the lookout at
botched badly done

If anybody does not believe that Mr. King was in the store, if they believe that Osvaldo Cruz, Lorelle Henry, and Bobo Evans are all lying, that the sale of the cigarettes to Mr. Bolden means nothing, then they should find him not guilty. I don't think that is possible. If anybody looking at this case believes that the store was not cased, that Mr. Harmon just "happened" to be at the drugstore, although now he says he doesn't remember where he was, then they should find him not guilty. I don't think that is possible, either. The truth of the matter is that Bobo Evans participated in a crime with Mr. Cruz, Mr. King, and Mr. Harmon.

They are all equally guilty. The one who grabbed the cigarettes, the one who wrestled for the gun, the one who checked the place to **see if the coast was clear**. What would have happened if Mr. Harmon had come out of that store and gone over to Mr. King and said, "There's someone in the store"? Perhaps they would have gone someplace else to carry out their "getover," or maybe they would have just **called it a day** and gone home. Steve Harmon was part of the plan that caused the death of

....

see if the coast was clear make sure nobody but Mr. Nesbitt
was in the store

called it a day given up; decided not to rob the place

Alguinaldo Nesbitt. I can imagine him trying to distance himself from the event. Perhaps, in some strange way, he can even say, as his attorney has suggested, that because he did not give a thumbs-up signal, or some sign to that effect, that he has successfully **walked the moral tightrope that relieves him of responsibility in this matter**. But Alguinaldo Nesbitt is dead, and his death was caused by these men.

Mr. King's attorney wants to distance Mr. King from the murder by attacking the character of the State's witnesses. But the fact of the matter is that Mr. Evans is an associate of Mr. King. If he had chosen priests and Boy Scouts as his companions, I'm sure we wouldn't be here today. But Mr. King cannot distance himself from the fact—the cold, hard fact—that a man is dead because of him.

Mr. Harmon wants us to look at him as a high school student and as a filmmaker. He wants us to think, well, he didn't pull the trigger. He didn't wrestle with Mr. Nesbitt. He wants us to believe that because he wasn't in the drugstore when the robbery went down, he

··

walked the moral tightrope that relieves him of responsibility in this matter convinced himself that he did not do anything wrong and should not be punished

wasn't involved. Again, perhaps he has even convinced himself that he wasn't involved.

But yes, Mr. Harmon was involved. He made a moral decision to participate in this "getover." He wanted to "get paid" with everybody else. He is as guilty as everybody else, no matter **how many moral hairs he can split**. His participation made the crime easier. His willingness to check out the store, no matter how poorly he did it, was one of **those causative factors** that resulted in the death of Mr. Nesbitt. None of us can bring back Mr. Nesbitt. None of us can restore him to his family. But you, you twelve citizens of our state, of our city, can bring a measure of justice to his killers.

And that's all I ask of you: to reach into your hearts and minds and **bring forth** that measure of justice. Thank you.

....

how many moral hairs he can split what he tells himself about what is right and what is wrong

those causative factors the things

bring forth carry out

BEFORE YOU MOVE ON...

1. **Summarize** On pages 176–180, how does Briggs try to persuade the jury that King is not guilty?

2. **Comparisons** How are the closing arguments that O'Brien and Petrocelli give different from each other?

LOOK AHEAD Read pages 197–209 to see if the jury finds Steve innocent or guilty.

CUT TO: EXTERIOR: COURTROOM. The doors of the court are closed as the camera nears it. The door is pushed open and we see the INTERIOR of the COURTROOM. We see the JURY turned toward the JUDGE, who speaks in a quiet, almost fatherly manner. We hear his voice as the camera seems to settle down on a seat. STEVE, sensing that a friend has arrived, turns and tries to smile at MR. SAWICKI but cannot manage it through his nervousness.

We look around the COURTROOM as the JUDGE's voice **drifts in and out**.

JUDGE: If you believe that Mr. King was a participant in the robbery, whether he actually pulled the trigger or not, you must return a verdict of Guilty. If you believe . . . (Voice fades out.)

CUT TO: **Stuart portrait** of George Washington on right wall.

CUT TO: New York State flag. Then: American flag.

CUT TO: **Motto** over desk.

JUDGE: . . . that Mr. Harmon did go into the store with the purpose of . . . (Voice fades out.) without regard to who actually pulled the trigger . . .

....

drifts in and out is quiet, then loud
Stuart portrait A famous painting
Motto Saying, Quotation

CUT TO: **Wall mural.**

CUT TO: JURY.

CUT TO: CU of JUDGE.

JUDGE: Then you must return a verdict of
Guilty of felony murder.

Camera, from POV of STEVE's MOTHER, swings wildly around the
room, stopping momentarily at those symbols that fill the
COURTROOM. Throughout this time the last words of the judge are
repeated.

JUDGE: Then you must return a verdict of
Guilty of felony murder.

Then you must return a verdict of Guilty of
felony murder.

Then you must return a verdict of Guilty of
felony murder. . . .

FADE OUT.

FADE IN: STEVE in CELL. For the first time JAMES KING is in the
cell with him. KING leans against wall, still dressed in the clothes
he wore at the trial.

....

Wall mural. Large painting covering the wall.

KING: How you doing? You scared?

STEVE: Yeah. You?

KING (subdued): **Naw, ain't nothing to it. If the man wants you, he got you.** Ain't nothing to it, man.

GUARD: Hey, we **got a pool going**. I bet you guys get life without the possibility of parole. The guys on the next block think you're going to get 25 to life. You guys want in on it?

CUT TO: STEVE. He looks away, then buries his face in his hands.

CUT TO: GUARD. He is smirking.

GUARD: That a yes or a no?

CUT TO: Two YOUNG MEN, handcuffed together, being led to the next cell. One looks terrified. The other is **putting on a show of bravado**.

GUARD: You guys treat me nice, and I'll put in a word for you up at Greenhaven. Maybe I can get you a boyfriend that's really built.

....

Naw, ain't nothing to it. If the man wants you, he got you.
No. If the legal system wants you in jail, you will go to jail.

got a pool going are betting money

putting on a show of bravado trying to look brave

CUT TO: STEVE in the MESS HALL. He avoids looking at KING. There is a **shoving match** down from where he sits. An inmate reaches over and takes STEVE's meat with a fork. STEVE looks up and sees the taker looking at him menacingly. He looks down at the tray.

CUT TO: STEVE in CELL. Outside the cell there is a clock on the wall with a wire guard over it. The second hand moves slowly.

CUT TO: INMATES enjoying a domino game as if they are far away from the prison, in some friendly setting.

....

shoving match fight

Last night I was afraid to go to sleep. It was as if closing my eyes was going to cause me to die. There is nothing more to do. There are no more arguments to make. Now I understand why so many of the guys who have been through it before, who have been away to prison, keep talking about appeals. They want to continue the argument, and the system has said that it is over.

My case **fills me**. When I left the courtroom after the judge's instructions to the jury, I saw Mama **clinging** to my father's arm. There was a look of **desperation** on her face. For a moment I felt sorry for her, but I don't anymore. The only thing I can think of is my case. I listen to guys talking about appeals and I am already planning mine.

Every word that has been said in court is burned into my brain. "Steve Harmon made a moral decision," Ms. Petrocelli said. I think about December of last year. What was the decision I made? To walk down

....

fills me is all that I think about
clinging holding on tightly
desperation hopelessness, fear

the streets? To get up in the morning? To talk to King? What decisions did I make? But I don't want to think about decisions, just my case. Nothing is real around me except the panic. The panic and the movies that dance through my mind. I keep **editing** the movies, making the scenes right. **Sharpening the dialog.**

"A getover? I don't do getovers," I say in the movie in my mind, my chin tilted slightly upward. "I know what right is, what truth is. **I don't do tightropes,** moral or otherwise."

I **put strings** in the background. Cellos. Violas.

....

editing changing
Sharpening the dialog. Rewriting what people say.
I don't do tightropes I have never told lies about things I did
put strings add music

GUARD: King! Harmon! You got a verdict! Let's go!

CUT TO: COURTROOM, now fairly crowded. O'BRIEN is talking to JUDGE. She finishes and sits down next to STEVE.

O'BRIEN: They got a verdict this morning. They've just been waiting for the Nesbitt family to arrive.

STEVE: What do you think?

O'BRIEN: They have a verdict. I hope it's one we want to hear. No matter what it is, we can **continue your case**. We can appeal. You okay?

STEVE: No.

JUDGE: Is everybody here? Is everybody here?

CLERK: I think so.

JUDGE: Prosecution ready?

PETROCELLI: Ready.

JUDGE: Defense?

CUT TO: CU of O'BRIEN.

....

continue your case keep arguing that you are not guilty

O'BRIEN: Ready.

CUT TO: CU of JUDGE.

JUDGE: Bring in the jury.

Very LS as WORDS roll slowly over the screen as in the beginning.

This *is* the true story of
Steve Harmon.
This *is* the story of his
life
and of his
trial.

(We see the jury members taking their places in the jury box.)

It was not an episode that he expected.

It was not the life or activity that he thought

would fill every bit of his soul or

change what life meant to him.

(The JUDGE has read the verdicts and hands them to the CLERK as GUARDS stand behind the DEFENDANTS.)

He has transcribed *the* images and *conversations* as he remembers them.

The color begins to fade as the JURY FOREMAN reads verdicts. Two GUARDS begin to put handcuffs on JAMES KING as color changes to black and white. It is clear that the JURY has found him guilty. We see KING being taken from the COURTROOM.

We see **JURY FOREMAN** as he continues to read.

CUT TO: CU of STEVE's MOTHER. We see her desperately clasping her hands before her, her face distorted with the tension of the moment, then suddenly, dramatically, she lifts her hands high and closes her eyes.

CUT TO: The GUARDS who were standing behind STEVE move away from him. He has been found not guilty. STEVE turns toward

....

JURY FOREMAN the person in charge of the jury

O'BRIEN as camera closes in and film grows grainier. STEVE spreads his arms to hug O'BRIEN, but she stiffens and turns to pick up her papers from the table before them.

CUT TO: CU of O'BRIEN. Her lips tense; she is **pensive**. She gathers her papers and moves away as STEVE, arms still outstretched, turns toward the camera. His image is in black and white, and the grain is nearly broken. It looks like one of the pictures they **use for psychological testing, or some strange beast**, a monster.

The image **freezes** as last words roll and stop mid screen.

A Steve Harmon Film

....

pensive thinking seriously about something

use for psychological testing, or some strange beast show people to see how they think about things, or a strange animal

freezes stops

It is five months since the trial, almost a year, **minus** a few days, since the robbery in the drugstore. James King was sentenced to 25 years to life. Osvaldo was arrested for stealing a car and sent to **a reformatory**. As far as I know, Bobo is still in jail.

My mother doesn't understand what I am doing with the films I am making. I have been taking movies of myself. In the movies I talk and tell the camera who I am, what I think I am about. Sometimes I set the camera up outside and walk up to it from different angles.

Sometimes I set the camera up in front of a mirror and film myself as a reflection. I wear different clothes and sometimes try to change my voice. Jerry likes to use the camera, and I let him film me, too. Whatever I do pleases my mother, because I am here with her and not put away in some jail.

After the trial, my father, with tears in his eyes, held me close and said that he was thankful that I did

----

minus if you take away; subtracting

a reformatory a school that helps teenage criminals change their lives for the better

not have to go to jail. He moved away, and **the distance between us seemed to grow bigger and bigger.** I understand the distance. My father is no longer sure of who I am. He doesn't understand me even knowing people like King or Bobo or Osvaldo. He wonders what else he doesn't know.

That is why I take the films of myself. I want to know who I am. I want to know the **road to panic that I took.** I want to look at myself a thousand times to look for one true image. When Miss O'Brien looked at me, after we had won the case, what did she see that caused her to turn away?

What did she see?

....

the distance between us seemed to grow bigger and bigger
I could tell he no longer thought I was the same person

road to panic that I took reasons I did the things I did and how close I came to being in jail forever

BEFORE YOU MOVE ON...
1. **Conclusions** On page 207, O'Brien is not friendly to Steve when the trial is over even though he is found innocent. Why not?

2. **Character** Reread pages 208–209. How has Steve changed because of the trial?